BLACK GIRL, WHITE GIRL

AN INSPECTOR HENRY TIBBETT MYSTERY

BLACK GIRL,
WHITE GIRL

Patricia Moyes

An Owl Book

HENRY HOLT AND COMPANY / NEW YORK

Copyright © 1989 by Patricia Moyes
All rights reserved, including the right to reproduce
this book or portions thereof in any form.
Published by Henry Holt and Company, Inc.,
115 West 18th Street, New York, New York 10011.
Published in Canada by Fitzhenry & Whiteside Limited,
195 Allstate Parkway, Markham, Ontario L3R 4T8.

Library of Congress Cataloging-in-Publication Data
Moyes, Patricia.
Black girl, white girl / by Patricia Moyes.—1st ed.
p.   cm—(A Henry Holt mystery)
ISBN 0-8050-1148-X
ISBN 0-8050-1149-8 (An Owl Book: pbk.)
I. Title.
PR6063.O9B49   1989
823'.914—dc20   89-7440
                                                    CIP

Henry Holt books are available at special discounts
for bulk purchases for sales promotions, premiums,
fund-raising, or educational use. Special editions
or book excerpts can also be created to specification.

For details contact:
Special Sales Director
Henry Holt and Company, Inc.
115 West 18th Street
New York, New York 10011

First published in hardcover by
Henry Holt and Company, Inc., in 1989.

First Owl Book Edition—1990

Designed by Paula R. Szafranski
Printed in the United States of America
3 5 7 9 10 8 6 4 2

1

Christmas Eve in London. Not one of those merry, glittering, snow-spattered Christmas Eves, but a dark, dank one with intermittent sleety rain. However, Henry Tibbett—Chief Superintendent Tibbett of the C.I.D.—and his wife, Emmy, were feeling cheerful enough. It was a tradition that on Christmas Eve they dined at the house of friends in the City of London. The dinner and the company had been as good as ever, putting the Tibbetts into an excellent frame of mind as they drove home through the deserted streets of London's business quarter, a mildly festive West End, and then down the never-sleeping clamor of the King's Road toward The World's End. For those not familiar with London, it should perhaps be pointed out that this address is not as dire as it sounds. The World's End is a pub, which for decades marked the dividing line between chic, artistic Chelsea and working-class Fulham. This distinction has now disappeared. In the sixties and seventies, houses well west of The World's End were described by house agents as being in Chelsea. Now that Fulham is fashionable, whereas Chelsea is considered somewhat brash, the same houses have reverted in the property advertisements to where they have always belonged—the Borough of Fulham.

The Tibbetts had left their friends at half past eleven, so by the time they had parked the car and Emmy had the key in the lock, it was already Christmas Day, by one minute—and the telephone was ringing.

"I'll take it," Henry said. "Hope to God it's not an emergency." He picked up the receiver from the hall table. "Tibbett here."

"Henry! Happy Christmas!" The voice was low-pitched, could be masculine or feminine. Henry thought for a moment that he recognized it, then put the idea out of his head as too farfetched. The voice went on, "I've been trying to get you all the evening, but there was no reply. I thought for a moment you might be out of town."

"Who's speaking?"

"You don't know? Shame on you, Henry." The voice chuckled.

Henry said, "If I didn't know it was impossible . . . can it be Lucy?"

"Of course it's Lucy, you silly man. Lucy Pontefract-Deacon." This, being a typically English surname, is pronounced "Pomfrey-Doon."

"My dear Lucy—where are you? You should be in Tampica, enjoying the sun."

"Well, I'm not. I'm in London, enjoying the rain, and trying to get in touch with you."

"I'm sorry, Lucy. We were out to dinner. When shall we see you?"

"As soon as possible, young man. I suppose you're busy over Christmas?"

"No, not really. We had our celebration dinner this evening. We'd planned to spend tomorrow quietly—Emmy's going to make my favorite lunch."

"What's that?"

"Steak-and-kidney pudding. Would you like to join us?"

"Steak-and-kidney pudding!" Miss Pontefract-Deacon

2

seemed to be licking the words. "I don't suppose I've tasted one in sixty years. Not the right sort of fare for Tampica, but for London in December . . . thank you, Henry. What time? I need to talk to you."

"Then come around noon. Where are you staying?"

"A rather grim and expensive hotel in Kensington. They promise a festive lunch for tomorrow, which I fear means frozen turkey and balloons. Expect me at noon. My love to Emmy." The line went dead.

Emmy said, "I heard some of that. Is it really Lucy?"

"It's really Lucy," Henry assured her. "She's come all the way from the Caribbean to spend Christmas at what she calls a grim and expensive Kensington hotel. She must finally have gone crazy in her old age."

Emmy smiled. "Lucy may be nearly ninety, but we both know that she's far from crazy. You'll find she has a good reason for coming to London."

"But what?" Henry was talking more or less to himself. "She seems very anxious to speak to me—or to us. Why couldn't she have telephoned from Tampica? Why come all this way?"

"Well," said Emmy, "we'll find out tomorrow. Or rather, today. Happy Christmas, darling."

At twelve noon on Christmas Day, freezing rain was falling, thin but penetrating, as a taxi bearing Lucy Pontefract-Deacon pulled up outside the Victorian house where the Tibbetts lived in their ground-floor apartment. The old lady climbed out with a certain amount of difficulty, her voluminous tweed skirt and tentlike raincoat hampering her progress. She opened an enormous handbag and fumbled in its interior while the cabby sat waiting with patient resignation. At last, Miss Pontefract-Deacon came up with a fistful of coins that seemed to satisfy her. She handed them to the driver.

"Merry Christmas to you!"

The driver did not return the greeting. He counted the coins, slammed the taxi into gear, and roared away in obvious disgust.

Henry already had the front door open and he hurried down the steps to meet his visitor. It was six years since he had seen Lucy, and even then she had been over eighty. It seemed incredible that she should have left the tropical island of Tampica, where she had spent almost all her life, to come to London in midwinter. She had not changed much, Henry thought. A little frailer, a little thinner—but her wrinkled, suntanned face was as merry as ever, her eyes as bright, and her back as ramrod straight. She grasped Henry's outstretched hand in both of hers and kissed him on the cheek.

"My dear Henry! How good to see you! No, no, I can manage the steps perfectly well, thank you. What a surly fellow that cabdriver was. And I gave him a two-shilling tip."

Henry smiled. "What you call two shillings is only ten p.," he remarked, "and I'm afraid it doesn't buy much these days."

"Oh, I get so confused with these newfangled pence!" Lucy exclaimed. "And now I'm told that they're not printing any more pound notes. Just these horrible little coins, which appear to be worth practically nothing. I can remember when a pound was a pound. Ah, Emmy! How splendid you look, my dear! Just as young as ever, and I believe you've lost weight."

"You always were the soul of tact, Lucy." Emmy returned the old lady's kiss. "Now, come in and have a drink, and tell us all about Tampica, and what brings you here."

Lucy divested herself of her raincoat, accepted a sherry, and established herself in the largest armchair. Then she said, raising her glass, "A very happy Christmas to you both."

4

"And to you, Lucy." Henry clinked his glass against hers. "Rather different from Christmas in Tampica."

"Yes." Lucy sounded serious. "And I don't only mean the climate."

"Oh, dear," said Emmy. "Trouble?"

"I fear so." Lucy took a sip, then put down her glass. She turned to Henry. "You remember Eddie Ironmonger?"

"I'm not likely to forget him in a hurry," said Henry. "I heard he'd been elected Prime Minister of Tampica, as everybody expected. I hope he's not—"

Lucy interrupted. "Yes, he was elected when Sam Drake-Frobisher resigned, quite shortly after Independence. He served out Sam's term, and then was reelected for another four years. I need hardly say that he made a very fine Prime Minister."

"I'm sure he did." Henry was remembering the handsome, urbane lawyer-turned-politician, whom he had known as Tampican Ambassador to the United States.

"Did he marry again?" Emmy asked. It had been in connection with Lady Ironmonger's tragic death that the Tibbetts had met Sir Edward.

Lucy shook her head. "No. It's funny, isn't it? With all her faults, nobody could replace Mavis." There was a small pause, as all three remembered. Then Lucy became brisk. "Well," she said, "you know the workings of democracy as well as I do. Remember what GBS said? 'Democracy substitutes election by the incompetent many for appointment by the corrupt few.' That may have been a little harsh, but the fact remains that politicians wishing to get elected slur over hard facts and make empty promises. And at the same time, the electorate demands miracles from its leaders and throws them out when they fail to deliver."

"You mean they threw Sir Edward out?" Henry was surprised.

"Eddie," said Lucy, "was much too honest to promise miracles. Every island in the Caribbean has got horrific economic problems, and Tampica is no exception. Eddie managed to keep things moving slowly towards solvency while he was in office, but his policies of austerity weren't popular. So you can imagine what happened two years ago, when he campaigned on slogans like 'Tighten our belts and work harder.' Of course they threw him out."

"So I suppose he's leader of the opposition now," said Emmy.

"No, no. He actually lost his seat in Parliament and retired from politics. Well—almost. He's now Governor-General— the titular head of state of Tampica, and with as little political power as our own dear Queen."

"I feel very remiss," Henry said. "I haven't kept up with Tampican affairs. Who is the present Prime Minister?"

Promptly, Lucy replied, "A very unsavory little man by the name of Chester Carruthers. I'm sure you never met him. He promised the people health, wealth, and prosperity—and of course they fell for it."

"He must have been in office for two years already," Emmy pointed out. "Surely the voters must be disillusioned by now. I was reading somewhere the other day about Tampica's economy being in bad trouble."

Lucy sighed. "You two have been away from the Caribbean for too long. Perhaps you don't even know that some states in our part of the world have two economies."

"Two economies?"

"I fear so. The official economy and the drug economy."

"Oh, my God." Henry was profoundly depressed. "Like the Seawards affair?"

"Much worse, I'm afraid. The Seawards affair, as you call it, was nipped in the bud. The Seaward Islands are still a crown colony with internal self-rule, their economy is very healthy, and the drug problem is minimal. Why, you ask? I'll tell you. Because the government was never involved."

"And this man Carruthers is?"

Lucy looked straight at Henry. "Eddie and I are almost certain. He, and some other members of his cabinet. That's why I am here."

"What do you expect me to do?" Henry made a hopeless gesture.

Ignoring him, Lucy went on. "It's Mafia money, of course. Enormous quantities of it. That's the drug economy, and Chester the Creep is making sure it goes to the people who can keep him in power. He also knows who his enemies are."

"You and Sir Edward," said Emmy.

Lucy smiled. "Why do you think I am here? Why do you imagine I didn't simply write or telephone? Because Eddie and I are—to put it bluntly—afraid."

"I can't believe it." Henry was remembering the lovely island, the friendly people, the heady excitement of independence, the growing tourist industry. "What could happen to you, of all people, Lucy? Or to Sir Edward, come to that."

"Mail is being tampered with," Lucy replied calmly, "and telephone lines tapped. People opposed to the government are meeting with unaccountable accidents. Even obeah—or the threat of it—is being used. There is no West Indian, however westernized, who doesn't dread the obeah-man in his heart. To tell you all this, somebody had to come to England. Eddie had no ostensible reason for coming, and if he had done so, he would be in considerable danger when he went back. I, on the other hand, am well known to be of British origin, even though I have taken Tampican nationality,

7

as you know. I put it out that I wanted to visit members of my family in England, while I could still make the journey; that I wished to see my ancestral home again for the last time, and other such nonsense. Also, I am not scared of obeah-men. So my trip, although it may not be popular in some circles, is at least regarded as harmless."

"That's all very well." Henry sounded thoughtful. "But I still don't see what you expect me to do."

"Just listen, for the moment." Lucy's bright blue eyes twinkled. "We've worked as a team before, Henry, and we can do it again."

"But vague suspicions aren't—"

Lucy held up her hand for silence. "Now pay attention, my dear. What I am going to say is very serious and far from vague. Eddie and I are both convinced that Carruthers is involved up to his neck in using the island as a transit post for drug running between South America and the States." She paused. "In fact, it's even possible that by now he wishes he could extricate himself, but things have gone too far. He's dead scared of his Mafia masters, and he also needs their money— not just to feather his own nest, but to keep him in office."

Henry said, "It's easy to see how he could take bribes, personally—but how does he arrange what you call the drug economy?"

Lucy smiled and shook her head sadly. "The indigenous population of Tampica isn't very large, you know. At any one time, I'd say that in round figures a third of the people on the island are Tampicans, another third are migrant workers from other islands, and a third are tourists. The down-islanders and tourists are transients and notice nothing—unless they want to lay hands on some drugs for their own use; in which case, they find it very much easier than the Draconian laws on our statute book would suggest. I hate to admit it, but this does no harm to our tourist trade. Also, we have a strict system of banking confidentiality, which may encourage the inflow of foreign capital, but is also extremely convenient for illicit deals."

"So just what happens?" Emmy asked. "I mean, suppose some South American drug baron pays this Carruthers a really whacking bribe. Take it from there."

"Simple, my dear. Carruthers stashes away his share and then distributes large sums to key people. Cabinet members, the Chief of Police, magistrates, and so on. They, in turn, distribute what they think fit to people under them whose help they need. Now, these people have naturally become prosperous, which gives them spending power at the restaurants, shops, and bars. In a tourist-oriented economy like ours, a great percentage of the population earns its living in these establishments. Tampica may appear poor on paper, but many people are doing very nicely, thank you." Lucy sighed. "I fear that any campaign to dry up this source of income would prove very unpopular. We can't rely on support from the island as a whole."

"I still don't see how I come in," Henry objected.

"Let us move from the general to the specific." Lucy was very firm. "There is on the island, at this very moment, an American whom Eddie and I are convinced is in the process of arranging a very big deal with Carruthers. Of course, he poses as an innocent tourist, and it would be not only very difficult but also dangerous for either of us to suggest anything else. Nevertheless, he is extraordinarily well in with Carruthers and his people. This does not match up with the idea of an ordinary tourist."

"What's his name?" Henry asked.

9

"He calls himself Thomas J. Brinkman." Lucy sniffed. "Goodness knows what his real name is. He's staying at Pirate's Cave, naturally. Only the best for Mr. Brinkman. Now, what Eddie and I need is proof positive that there is a deal brewing. With tape recordings, if possible. The sort of evidence that we could present to the United States, and that couldn't be suppressed."

"But—"

Lucy rolled comfortably over Henry's protest. "I said that it would be difficult for Eddie or myself to get this sort of evidence. But another ordinary tourist, staying in the same hotel, on holiday with—" she nodded toward Emmy—"with his charming wife—well, you can see that things would be different."

Henry laughed. "My dear Lucy, you must see that this is a ridiculous idea. For a start, I've no more leave due to me this year. To go on with, we couldn't possibly afford the fare to Tampica, let alone the prices at Pirate's Cave—not to mention the fact that we'd never get in. This is the high season. And what's more—"

"Just a moment, Henry. Naturally, we considered those things." She lifted her enormous handbag from the floor beside her chair, opened it, and took out an envelope. "Here are two round-trip air tickets, London to Tampica. I collected them from the travel agent yesterday." She handed the envelope to Emmy, and began rummaging in the bag again like Santa Claus with his sack of goodies. "Ah, here we are!" Another bulky envelope emerged. "A thousand pounds' worth of Tampican dollars. You may have heard that we now have our own currency?" Beaming, she held the envelope out to Henry. "This should see you through as pocket money. Reservations at Pirate's Cave are no problem, and there'll be no hotel bill to speak of."

"Don't be silly, Lucy. I can't possibly take it."

"Of course you can take it."

"Whose money is it, anyway?" Henry demanded.

Lucy said, "I am nearly ninety years old, Henry, and I am not a poor woman. Quite apart from anything else, you may remember that I made some very profitable land investments in Tampica. As a result, I own shares in both Barracuda Bay Hotel and Pirate's Cave. My own wants and needs are very modest. I have my house and garden and a faithful retainer. I don't need money. I need peace of mind."

"All the same—"

"And peace of mind can only be achieved, as far as I am concerned, by saving Tampica from the evil forces that are closing in on her. By offering you this trip, I am not doing you a favor. Far from it. By accepting it, you will be doing me one."

There was a silence. Henry and Emmy exchanged glances. Then Henry said, "Even if we did accept—what did you mean about no hotel bill to speak of?"

Lucy seemed to relax. She sat back in her chair and smiled broadly. "That's better. Naturally, the last thing we want is for you to be connected in any way with Eddie or me. However, the manager of Pirate's Cave is a good friend of mine. He will accommodate you and Emmy at the special rates reserved for the families of staff members. You would be surprised how low they are."

"Can you trust him?"

"Yes, Henry, I can." Lucy said no more, and Henry did not press the point.

"Okay so far, Lucy. But what about my leave?"

"My dear Henry, I may be a decrepit relic from a far country, but I do still have some friends. And so does Eddie, and so do the Barringtons—you remember the bishop and his

11

wife? Yes, it's the old Tampica gang assembled again, probably for the last time. I came to London via Washington."

"You saw the Barringtons?" Emmy's voice was warm with affection. "How are they?"

"Older," said Lucy. "Like all of us. But in good health and spirits. Prudence would like to revisit Tampica, but Matthew feels once one has retired, it is better to stay retired." She paused. "That's not true, of course. He feels that, in the present situation, his appearance on the island might cause suspicion."

"But ours would not?" Henry put in. "Won't anybody remember that we've been there before?"

"Nobody who matters." Lucy was brisk and firm. "At the time of the Ironmonger case, Carruthers and his crew were young men, away getting their higher education in England or the States. Besides, remember that you and Emmy were only on Tampica for a few days, and that you had no official connection with the case. Ostensibly, the whole thing was in the hands of Inspector Bartholomew—who is no longer with us."

"You mean, he's left the island?" Henry was remembering the tall, good-looking Detective-Inspector with whom he had worked.

"No," said Lucy, grimly. "I was employing a euphemism. He is dead."

"But he can't have been more than forty!" Emmy cried.

"Oh, he didn't die of natural causes, dear Emmy. He had just been promoted to Police Commissioner, and he telephoned me to say he was coming over the mountain to see me because he had suspicions about what might be going on in high government circles. His Jeep just happened to skid and go off the road and over the precipice. Curious, wasn't it?"

"That settles it," said Henry. "Thank you, Lucy. We accept. But what about my leave?"

"I think you will find no problem, my dear," said Lucy. "And now—did you say steak-and-kidney pudding?"

The day after the Christmas holiday period, Henry was unsurprised to be summoned to the office of the Assistant Commissioner at Scotland Yard.

"You wanted to see me, sir?"

"Yes, Tibbett. Sit down."

Henry sat while his boss fiddled with some papers.

"A rather curious situation has arisen, Tibbett. We have had an absolutely unofficial request for help from Tampica. The Caribbean island, you know. Used to be a colony, but independent now. Member of the Commonwealth, of course."

Henry continued to say nothing.

"They would like you to go out there for a few days—say a week—to look into . . . well . . ."

"Is this request from the Tampican government, sir?"

The Assistant Commissioner looked a little put out. "The request came to us through the Governor-General, Sir Edward Ironmonger. I understand you know him."

"Slightly, sir."

Suddenly, the A.C. grinned. "And I also understand that you know perfectly well what all this is about."

Henry grinned back. "Yes, sir."

"Then stop this stupid charade. Go on, get going, and good luck to you. Oh, by the way, you're on leave, as from today. You realize that this has nothing to do with us."

"Of course, sir. Nothing."

13

2

There are few sensations comparable to that of returning after a space of time to a place that has played a special part in one's life. On the following Sunday morning, Henry and Emmy, looking down on the green and gray landscape of Tampica from the jetliner that had brought them overnight from London, felt mixed emotions. Nostalgia, affection, and some apprehension. They wondered what they would find. Certainly many changes.

The first change was manifest in the fact that they were in a wide-bodied jet and not in an eight-seater Norman Islander. The airfield of Tampica had been enlarged out of all recognition, and the wooden huts and tiny bar replaced by a modern concrete complex of buildings. The central reception area proclaimed in beautifully carved wooden letters set against a wall of natural stone that this was TAMPICA—EDWARD IRONMONGER INTERNATIONAL AIRPORT. And a fat lot of use it is having an airport named after you, Emmy thought to herself, if you dare not come out into the open to fight a blatant evil. Clever of the Tampican government to turn Eddie into a folk hero; better than killing him, and almost as effective. But, fortunately, not quite. There would never be a Lucy Pontefract-Deacon International Airport.

The next change was in the Customs and Immigration

Department. Before, everything had been relaxed and informal. People knew each other as personal friends; and, while the formalities were observed, there were joking and inquiries about families and chit-chat about other islands, as the officials thumbed easily through passports. Now everything was brisk and efficient. Young men in immaculate white uniforms with gold epaulettes of rank scrutinized papers and passports with unamused severity, barked short questions about length of stay and temporary addresses, and wielded heavy metal stamps with the precision of pile drivers.

As the taxi drove away from the airport, Henry noticed Emmy's glum face and said, "Cheer up, love. It's progress, after all."

"Is it?" Emmy did not seem cheered. "Why does everything have to change? Look at that!"

They were driving through the island's principal town, Tampica Harbour. Trendy boutiques and cut-price liquor stores had proliferated, pushing out the little shops that had sold local fruit and vegetables. The streets were full of scantily dressed tourists, many of them presumably off the three large cruise liners, which the Tibbetts had noticed from the air, moored alongside the wharf at Barracuda Bay.

Henry said, "You can't put the clock back. And remember, Ironmonger himself was always in favor of developing mass tourism. The island has to live."

Emmy managed a smile. "Yes, I know it does. It's just that—"

"I know."

They drove on in silence, through the town and along the coast. Then Henry said, "Well, there's something that hasn't changed."

"What?"

"Pirate's Cave. It looks just the same as ever."

The taxi had turned into a driveway that ran between rolling green lawns and beautifully tended tropical trees and shrubs—oleander, hibiscus, plumeria, pride of Barbados, ginger thomas—all blooming in a gentle explosion of color. The taxi breasted a slight rise, and there, on the other side, was the hotel itself and the crescent of silver sand lapped by aquamarine sea that was its private beach. In the bay, protected by the encircling arm of the reef, little Sunfish dinghies with bright sails scudded on the water; on the beach, sun-browned bodies lay on the sand, like hot dogs on a bun. Nothing had changed.

A smiling porter with a luggage trolley was there to unload the Tibbetts' bags and accompany them to the reception desk. A beautiful black girl greeted them and told them the number of their cottage.

"We don't have keys," she explained. "But we do advise you to put all your money and important documents into a safe-deposit box. You won't need any money here—you just sign for everything. Of course, if you decide to go into town, you can always come and take out some cash."

Henry and Emmy signed up for a safe-deposit box on the spot, put their cash, tickets, and passports into it, and, with a marvelous sense of release, left the desk to follow their baggage through the gardens to their cottage.

Like almost all visitors arriving at a Caribbean resort, the Tibbetts' first thought was to get to the beach as fast as possible. Long before anything else was unpacked, swimsuits were extracted from suitcases, suntan lotion liberally applied, big striped towels whisked from the bathroom—and Henry and Emmy were running barefoot through the palm trees down the little sandy path that led from their cottage to the sea.

As they came out into the brilliant sunshine, Emmy stopped dead and pointed skyward. "What on earth is that?"

Henry, squinting upward, saw—some three hundred feet above—a parachutist apparently making a descent into the sea. The parachute itself was gaudily striped in red, white, and blue, and the human figure looked small and very vulnerable dangling from it. Dangling, but not descending. Instead, the parachute seemed to be moving on its own volition over the water, maintaining a steady height. It only took a split second to spot the slender line that connected the flier to a motorboat a couple of hundred feet ahead of him. The boat was moving—not at the high speed of a water-ski boat, but at a fairly leisurely pace, which kept the parachute full of wind and at a constant height.

As Henry put a hand up to shade his eyes for a better view, a voice beside him said, "That's parasailing, Mr. Tibbett. Our latest sport."

"Sir Edward!" Henry and Emmy both turned with delighted smiles to greet the tall black man who had apparently followed them from their cottage to the beach and now stood behind them, where the grove of trees met the open sand. He was not dressed for swimming, but wore blue cotton trousers and a loose white shirt. Six years had changed Sir Edward very little: a trace stouter, perhaps, with a becoming tinge of gray hair at the temples; otherwise, as handsome and urbane as ever.

"I'm delighted to see you both," he said. "Lucy told me you were arriving today, but I just missed you at your cottage. Do you mind if we go back there for a few minutes? We need to talk."

Sir Edward Ironmonger, Governor-General of Tampica, relaxed in a rattan armchair. "Sorry to drag you away from the

17

beach, Tibbett, but I didn't want to be seen talking to you. Not just yet, at any rate." He smiled and lit one of the big cigars that Henry and Emmy remembered from his days as Ambassador to Washington. "Lucy told you everything, I understand."

Henry said, "I don't know about everything, Sir Edward. She told us enough to make us extremely worried about this island."

Sir Edward puffed earnestly at his cigar until it was performing to his satisfaction. "The parasailor you just saw was the American Lucy mentioned: Thomas J. Brinkman. He has developed a fanatical enthusiasm for the sport. Not only does he enjoy himself, but the bird's-eye view from up there is very comprehensive. That's why I didn't want to talk to you on the beach. Incidentally, it has been possible to arrange matters so that he is occupying the other half of this cottage. I hope that may facilitate matters."

Henry said, "Can you tell me just why you and Lucy are so suspicious about this man?"

"Several reasons." Ironmonger took another puff. "He has never visited this island before, but as soon as he arrived he was on friendly terms with the men in the government whom we suspect. It's impossible not to conclude that he was expected. Then, he is on his own—no family or friends—which doesn't fit with the pattern of an ordinary tourist. Then—here I am repeating local gossip—somebody like him was due to turn up. Rumor—and my sources of rumor are pretty reliable—has it that Carruthers's previous deal of this sort has fallen through. I don't know why. Maybe Carruthers was too greedy, or the drug runners found a better route, or both. In any case, the word is that Carruthers and his cronies need a new deal, and they need money. Brinkman seems the obvious candidate."

Henry nodded. "That does make sense."

"So," Sir Edward went on, "I'll have to leave it to you. But please keep me up to date on any developments." He took a small notepad out of his pocket and scribbled something on it; then he tore off the top sheet and handed it to Henry. "If you need to speak with me privately, call that number. If you do call it, you had better identify yourself by a code name. Let's see—what about Scott? It's a common enough name, but easy for you to remember. Mr. Scott of Scotland Yard."

Emmy smiled. "Are these cloak-and-dagger precautions really necessary, Sir Edward?"

Very seriously, Ironmonger replied, "Why do you think Lucy came all the way to London to speak to you?"

"All right. You've convinced me. Meanwhile, are we supposed to know you? As Henry and Emmy Tibbett, I mean?"

"Lucy and I think it best if we meet by chance at dinner this evening. There will be talk of a brief acquaintance many years ago in Washington, which will be the excuse for me to invite you to my table. I shall be dining in the restaurant here with some friends."

"Lucy?" Henry frowned. "Is that wise?"

Sir Edward smiled and shook his head. "Not Lucy. Oh, dear me, no. My party will consist of local celebrities. Our Prime Minister, the Honourable Chester Carruthers. Our Police Commissioner, Desmond Kelly. Our Finance Minister, the Honourable Joseph Palmer. And their wives, of course. It will be a good opportunity for you to meet these people. Since I am a widower," he added, "and therefore have no hostess at Government House, it has become my custom to entertain here at Pirate's Cave, which has the best cuisine on the island. These Sunday-evening dinners with government members are quite usual. Also, there are frequently guests staying in the hotel whom I have known from my years in the United States and Europe. Nobody will think it strange if we recognize each other. Of course, you will not mention your profession."

"Of course," Henry agreed. "So what am I supposed to be?"

"Lucy and I talked it over. We think, a wealthy retired businessman."

"I know practically nothing about business," Henry objected.

"Never mind. The question of your profession may not come up. If it does, I shall let it be known discreetly that you made money in import-export. I will hint that you have valuable connections both in Europe and the States. That way, our politicians will be eager to cultivate you. They need legitimate investment of foreign currency as well as the other sort."

"I hope I'll be able to play the part," Henry said.

"Of course you will." Emmy was quite definite. "And I shall be an eccentric."

Sir Edward's eyebrows went up. "You, Mrs. Tibbett? Eccentric? In what way?"

Emmy explained. "If we're supposed to be so rich, how come I'm wearing clothes from Marks and Spencer, instead of Dior? How come I've got no jewelry apart from my engagement ring, which cost Henry twenty pounds thirty years ago? I'll either have to be distinctly odd, or not appear at all."

"I see what you mean," Sir Edward conceded.

"So," Emmy went on, "I shall be devoted to good works. Luckily, I do quite a lot of charity work in London, so I'll be able to make that stick." She grinned at Henry. "This is going to be rather fun."

———

After Sir Edward left, the Tibbetts went back to the beach. As they splashed lazily in the water, they noticed a big raft moored a couple hundred feet offshore. On it stood three black men: one in the center of the floating platform, the other two behind him, to the right and to the left. As they watched, the parasailing boat maneuvered carefully into position behind the raft and decreased speed. The brilliant parachute with its dangling passenger began to lose height. As the now slack tow rope passed over the raft, the central figure grabbed it and skillfully passed it through a block, to give a purchase and make an anchoring spot. Then he hauled on the rope, and in no time the parasailor's feet were touching the platform for a perfect landing. The parachute was quickly smothered by the other two men, and the rope unclipped from the flier's harness. The boatman hauled in the rope and brought the boat alongside the raft. Very soon, all four men were on board and roaring cheerfully toward the shore.

Emmy said, "It must be wonderful. Parasailing, I mean. Are you going to try it?"

"Certainly not," Henry assured her. "Old age has a few privileges."

"You're not *that* old."

"I'm old enough to have a lot of gray hairs and to pass for a retired businessman. Anyhow, I've never been an athlete, as you know. I love snorkeling and a little decorous snow skiing and sailing boats. But I'm past the stage when I'm prepared to risk my neck at a crazy sport like that."

"Oh, I'm sure it's quite safe, Henry."

"All right, you go up if you want to. Only don't expect sympathy from me if things go wrong."

"I don't see what could go wrong."

"You will if you try it," said Henry, ominously.

The Tibbetts did not arrive in the dining room for dinner until after half past eight that evening. In conformity with the relaxed elegance of Pirate's Cave, Emmy wore a long wrap-around skirt of brightly printed cotton with a plain white blouse, and Henry had put on plaid seersucker trousers and a loose blue overshirt with white embroidery and kangaroo-pouch pockets. Like it or not, Henry had long since decided, there are uniforms everywhere. Anything more formal would have looked silly, but anything less formal would have caused slightly raised eyebrows.

Most of the hotel guests were finishing dinner, but Sir Edward Ironmonger's party was still lapping up soup. Henry and Emmy were shown to a table for two, overlooking the sea.

Sir Edward's table was large, circular, and centrally placed. Apart from the Governor-General himself, there were six guests, three men and three women, all black—but in skin shades varying from Sir Edward's own shining ebony to the pale café au lait of one of the ladies. Conversation at the table was lively, interspersed with much laughter. Waiters hovered with damask-wrapped bottles of wine. Every eye in the dining room was focused on the party, but the diners seemed quite unaware of the fact. Emmy had once—in her capacity as head of a charitable organization—attended an enormous garden party at Buckingham Palace. She had never forgotten the sight of the royal family calmly enjoying their tea in an open marquee, while thousands of goggling spectators watched every move of cup to lip, every regal mouthful of chocolate cake. This reminded her of that occasion.

As Henry and Emmy sat down, a solitary diner at the next

table put down his coffee cup and rose to leave. He was unmistakably American, in his forties, bronzed, athletic, and with sleek black hair and a slightly swarthy complexion. American-Italian, probably. The Tibbetts did not remember seeing him in the restaurant at lunchtime. As he passed Sir Edward's table on his way out, the Governor-General said, very audibly, "Good evening, Mr. Brinkman."

Brinkman did not reply. He simply nodded, giving no sign of recognition to anybody else in the party, and left the room. His broad back view gave the impression that he was shouldering his way through a crowd, although there was nobody to impede his progress. He disappeared into the shadows beyond the terrace.

Henry and Emmy began their meal. Couple by couple, the other diners departed, until only Sir Edward's party remained. Just as Emmy finished the last spoonful of her chocolate mousse, Sir Edward, slewing round in his chair to hail a waiter, appeared to see the Tibbetts for the first time.

"Goodness me," he boomed genially, "I can't be mistaken, can I? You *are* Henry Tibbett? And Mrs. Tibbett?"

Henry half-rose and bowed. "Sir Edward—what a good memory you have. I hesitated to—"

"Come over and join us for coffee and a liqueur." Sir Edward beamed. "Waiter, bring two more chairs. Come along, come along."

As the Tibbetts approached the round table, which was being deftly rearranged to accommodate two more, Sir Edward turned to his guests. "I met Mr. and Mrs. Tibbett some years ago in Washington, when I was in the embassy. He was negotiating some weighty deal between his London company and the States. I had no idea they were vacationing here. Allow me to present you . . ."

The three men pushed back their chairs and stood up. Beautiful manners, thought Emmy.

Ironmonger went on. "Mr. Henry Tibbett . . . Mrs. Tibbett . . . Our Prime Minister, Chester Carruthers, and Mrs. Carruthers." One of the men held out his hand. His smooth, round face seemed creased into a perpetually welcoming smile. At his side, the café-au-lait lady bowed her lovely head slightly in gracious acknowledgment. Her features were fine and delicate, her ancestry clearly mixed. Looking at her, Emmy felt a pang of shame at her own rather slapdash toilette. Mrs. Carruthers was exquisitely groomed, not a shining hair out of place, her makeup impeccable, with blue-shadowed eyelids and smoothly manicured hands with nails exactly matching her deep red lipstick.

"And this," Sir Edward went on, "is our Minister of Finance, Joe Palmer, and Mrs. Palmer." Two more hands were shaken. Palmer was an enormous, very black man, with crinkly hair and a dour expression. Mrs. Palmer was a large, flowing lady in a large, flowing dress, and her smile was easy and very sweet.

"And finally, our Police Commissioner, Desmond Kelly, and Mrs. Kelly." The Police Commissioner was tall, thin, and almost as pale in color as Mrs. Carruthers. He sported a neat moustache, and his manner was as clipped and correct as that of a caricatured colonial Englishman. As for his wife, she was a tiny black woman—almost invisible, it seemed to Emmy, sitting in the shadows in a dark green dress. As she extended her little bird's-claw hand, the only thing about her that was impossible to miss was the huge gold pectoral in the shape of a sunburst, which dwarfed her thin neck.

"And now, sit down and tell us what you would like to drink." Sir Edward settled back in his chair and lit one of his

24

inevitable cigars. "You don't object if I smoke, Mrs. Tibbett? No, I remember you don't . . . Waiter!"

Orders were given and served, and conversation became general. Emmy, who found herself sitting next to the lovely Mrs. Carruthers, soon discovered that the latter's first name was Carmelita and, rather surprisingly, that they had a common interest in voluntary charitable work. Emmy was soon listening, fascinated, to an account of Carmelita's efforts to set up day-care centers in Tampica; in turn she described her work as a hospital visitor in London. Henry, thinking it wiser to stay off any subjects connected with police matters, got into a discussion of the island's economy with the melancholy Mr. Palmer.

"Your tourist industry is obviously very healthy," Henry remarked.

Palmer sighed. "This is the high season. Don't forget, Mr. Tibbett, that we have to survive the whole year on the proceeds of just a few months."

"But your climate—" Henry checked himself. He was not supposed to know too much about Tampica's climate. "According to my travel agent, your climate is just about perfect all the year round. Can't you promote your off-season?"

"Naturally we try. But remember that the summer months are very pleasant in other parts of the world—the northern United States and Europe, for example. It is in the winter that the tourists desire to escape from bad weather."

It occurred to Henry that Palmer spoke English like a carefully learned foreign language. Remembering other Tampicans he had known, he felt reasonably sure that under stress the Honourable Minister would revert to island patois. Just another instance of the difficulty of adapting to public office and life on the international scene.

On Henry's left, the huge, merry Mrs. Palmer fanned herself with her menu card. She said, "De t'ing be, Mr. Tibbett, dat heah be jus' overhot, summertime. Overhot." Palmer looked sharply at his wife, as if in reproof, but she rolled comfortably on. "People say dis an' dat 'bout de 'conomy, but we doan do bad. No, we doan do bad. Is a good job Joe doin'."

From the far side of the table, Chester Carruthers said, "Just what is your business, Mr. Tibbett?"

Henry smiled. "I have no business at the moment, Mr. Prime Minister. I'm retired—and thankful for it."

"Very well, then. What was it?"

Hoping it came out smoothly, Henry said, "Trading, Mr. Carruthers. Buying and selling in various countries. It's often called import-export, but it really just means being a middle-man."

"And your commodities?" Carruthers's voice was sharp, although his smile never wavered.

Sir Edward came to the rescue. "Mr. Tibbett had interests in many fields. If I remember rightly, it was to do with domestic heating appliances that you were in Washington?"

"You remember correctly, as always, Sir Edward." Henry was profoundly grateful. Domestic heating appliances were something that nobody in Tampica could possibly know anything about.

Sir Edward went on. "Well, we're delighted to see you both on our island. Will you be staying long?"

"Until I hear from my friends in England that the weather has improved—always provided that Pirate's Cave can keep us." Henry smiled, to indicate that this was a pleasantry. Pirate's Cave, he implied, would always find room for such a wealthy customer. He was gratified to see that the point was

26

taken. A quick look of complete understanding passed between Carruthers and Palmer.

Palmer said, "If it would amuse you, Mr. Tibbett, I would
be delighted to take you and your wife on a tour of the island.
We have much of interest to show you. Interest, and perhaps
even opportunity."

"We should be honored," said Henry.

And so, over a final cup of coffee, it was arranged that the
Honourable Joseph Palmer, Minister of Finance, should call
for the Tibbetts at the hotel at ten o'clock the following
morning, and show them how Tampica was—as he put
it—striding boldly into the future. Mrs. Palmer roared with
laughter at the idea that she might join the expedition, but
invited Henry and Emmy to lunch afterward.

"An' you an' Carmelita, Chester—you come 'long too.
'Bout one o'clock. And doan you say you too busy, 'cos I
knows better." She laughed uproariously again, bestowed an
inexplicable wink on Emmy, and rose to her feet with the
majesty of a Spanish galleon setting sail. The party was over.

It was only later that Henry realized that neither the Police
Commissioner, Desmond Kelly, nor his little wife had said a
word.

3

he next morning, the Tibbetts were on the beach by nine o'clock, eager for a swim before their expedition. Not many of the hotel guests had arrived yet, but the indefatigible Mr. Brinkman was already on the parasailing raft, being helped into the black strapping harness. As Henry and Emmy swam lazily in shallow water near the shore, the boat revved up, and the gaudy parachute caught the breeze and lifted Brinkman gently aloft. Emmy saw the boatman making hand signals to his flying passenger, and in response Brinkman shifted the position of his hands slightly on the straps, bringing the parachute into a better alignment.

Since there was nobody remotely within earshot, Emmy felt that there was no harm in saying, "Well, he hasn't done anything very sinister yet. He hardly ever seems to have his feet on the ground."

"Lucy and Sir Edward have good reason to suspect him." Henry flipped over onto his back and floated on the buoyant salty water, watching the parachute far above him. "All the same, it's not going to be easy to get the evidence they need. I doubt if he'll use his cottage here as a rendezvous."

"And even if he does," Emmy pointed out, "there's no real communication between his suite and ours."

The guest cottages at Pirate's Cave, as the Tibbetts had discovered on their previous visit, were so arranged that each little building housed two suites, mirror images of each other. The two verandas were separated by a screening wall, but it was possible to hear what was being said on the adjoining porch. However, it was hardly likely that Brinkman and Carruthers would hold a secret meeting outside, and the interiors of the cottages were soundproofed to ensure perfect privacy.

"Oh, well." Henry was philosophical. "It's early days yet. We'd better go and get ready for our outing."

Promptly at ten o'clock, the Tibbetts—casually but neatly dressed—were waiting under the big tamarind tree at the entrance to Pirate's Cave. At a quarter past ten, they were still waiting. At half past ten, Emmy said, "We didn't misunderstand, did we? I mean, Mr. Palmer was going to pick us up here at ten?"

Henry laughed. "We've been away from here too long, as Lucy said. Have you forgotten about Caribbean time?"

"Of course not. But after all, he's a government minister."

"I don't think that makes very much difference."

It was twenty minutes to eleven when a big black car slid smoothly up to the tamarind tree. It was driven by a uniformed chauffeur, and in the back seat Joe Palmer creased his face into a welcoming smile, as if it hurt him to do so. The chauffeur jumped out and opened both front and back doors.

Palmer said, "Ah, good morning, Mr. Tibbett . . . Mrs. Tibbett . . . how punctual you are. . . . Now, I suggest that Mrs. Tibbett should ride in front, and if you will come in the back with me, sir, I shall be able to show you points of interest."

The tour was thorough and expertly conducted. Henry and

Emmy were shown the high-rise hotel at Barracuda Bay, catering to a less affluent market than Pirate's Cave. Then came a quick visit to a new beachside camping site, where backpackers could enjoy Tampica on a shoestring.

"But what we need, Mr. Tibbett," said Palmer earnestly, as the car moved off again, "is something in between. A development of housekeeping cottages to attract young tourists with children. We have the site"—he leaned forward and said to the driver, "Take us to Frigate Bay, Benson," and, relaxing again, went on—"our trouble is capital. We need investors—men of foresight and goodwill, prepared to wait a few years in order to get a spectacular return on their money."

"I understand," said Henry gravely.

"Ah, here we are." The car had stopped at the point where a rutted track ended at a grove of palm trees, which ringed a croissant-shaped beach. Palmer and the Tibbetts got out.

"You see?" Palmer waved an expressive arm. "Is this not a beautiful site? Can you not imagine the cottages grouped among the palms around the beach?"

"It's a long way from any shops," Emmy pointed out.

"Ah, Mrs. Tibbett, we have thought of that. We intend to build a small shopping mall—commissary, drugstore, gift shop, bar, and so on. This is all government property, you see. We plan to do the building, and then lease premises to qualified people. All we need is the capital investment. When that is forthcoming—"

Palmer broke off suddenly. "Well," he said, "I think we have seen enough here. There are many other things . . . come please . . ." His face had resumed its customary expression of displeased melancholy. He took Emmy's arm and almost hustled her back to the waiting car.

So the island tour progressed. The Tibbetts were shown a large, flat, unattractive tract of land where the government hoped—if foreign investors would cooperate—to set up small factories producing light industrial goods under license. They were invited to view and admire the enlarged Edward Ironmonger Airport. ("But even now it is only marginally big enough for jumbo jets. And we need better maintenance facilities and a bigger restaurant. . . .") They were taken to a hilltop beauty spot, with breathtaking views over the sapphire sea, and asked if it would not be improved by the addition of a bar and public lavatories. To this, Henry did not trust himself to reply.

In short, Joseph Palmer made it perfectly clear that there were dozens of opportunities for somebody like Henry to use his money in order to ruin Tampica for the enrichment of its citizens and himself. Henry was glad when Palmer glanced at his elegant gold watch and remarked that it was after twelve, and they should be getting back to lunch.

The Palmer residence was a substantial house standing on a hill overlooking the sweep of Pirate's Bay beach and the shimmering sea beyond. On the horizon, the dark humped shapes of other islands were just discernible on a clear day. The house was built in the usual manner of plastered concrete, with a wide terrace looking out to sea.

Approaching it up the winding drive, Emmy noticed what she had remarked before in the Caribbean—the wonderful, sure, and unexpected use of color on its exterior. Innate West Indian color sense could and did mix white, sky-blue, purple, and orange walls and shutters with stunning effect—and these same colors were echoed in the jacaranda, bougainvillea, and hibiscus flowering in the garden. And, all over again, on entering the house she felt the remembered pang of disap-

31

pointment at the cluttered, over-ornamented rooms, the penchant for garish plastic, the fussily patterned tiles on the floor. West Indians, as Emmy knew, are outside people. Only recently have some of the more affluent begun to consider the inside of a house as something more than a shelter from the rain and a place to sleep. And, given their climate, who can blame them?

The Tibbetts were swept up in a tide of welcome by the voluminous Mrs. Palmer ("You must call me Emmalinda, my dear. . . .") and ushered through the house and onto the terrace, where Chester and Carmelita Carruthers were already sipping drinks, leaning on the stone balustrade and looking down at the pinhead figures on the beach below. Rum punches were served all around by a soft-spoken young man who was introduced as one of the Palmers' sons: "Nathaniel, but we call him Prince."

As on the previous evening, Emmy soon found herself grouped with the other two women, while the men congregated at the far end of the terrace.

"I hope you enjoyed your tour, Mr. Tibbett." Carruthers smiled broadly at Henry. "Found something to interest you, I hope."

"I was interested in everything, Mr. Carruthers," said Henry, well aware that this was not the answer that the Prime Minister wanted.

"Yes, this is truly a land of opportunity. Joe will have explained that we are trying to broaden our economic base beyond tourism."

"Yes, so I gathered. I think you have great potential—if you can find the right investors."

"Ah, yes." Carruthers gave Henry a curious look. "The right investors, as you say."

Across the bay below, the white motorboat cut a foaming

white wake; and suspended in midair, level with the house, glided the multicolored parachute. Carruthers leaned over the balcony and waved. Not surprisingly, there was no answering greeting, for a parasailor's hands are fully occupied while in flight.

Henry said, "The indefatigible Mr. Brinkman, I presume."

"I have no idea." Carruthers's voice was cold, although he still smiled. "I am always glad to extend a friendly greeting to any tourist on our island."

"Of course," said Henry. And then, "Why, there's that boat again."

"What boat, Mr. Tibbett?" Carruthers was gazing out to sea.

"There—out beyond Pirate's Cave, just rounding the headland. The big motor cruiser with the dark blue hull."

There was a little pause. Then Carruthers said, "Yes, I see her. Why did you say 'again'?"

Henry turned to Palmer who, having refreshed his drink from the big jug on Prince's tray, came up at that moment. "You see her, Mr. Palmer? Isn't that the boat that was coming in to Frigate Bay just as we left this morning?"

"I am afraid I did not notice, Mr. Tibbett." He shaded his eyes and looked out to sea. "You mean the blue motorboat? Oh, she is often around. Belongs to some Americans, I believe. Boating is an important industry here, you know."

"I was just asking Mr. Tibbett which part of his tour had interested him the most," remarked Carruthers. "He seems to have found our island uniformly intriguing."

"In that case," said Palmer carefully, "it might perhaps be in order if we made a few modest suggestions. Always provided that Mr. Tibbett is amenable to the idea of some small investment."

Henry had a distinct impression of being trapped. The two

33

black men were standing on either side of him, talking across him as if he were not there. He said, "I am always interested in new and profitable investments, gentlemen, but I hardly feel I have seen enough of Tampica to—"

"Of course, of course." Carruthers was soothing. "While you are here, we will show you much, much more."

"The first thing one asks oneself before investing in a newly independent nation," Henry said blandly, "is—to be blunt—what of the political situation? Is it stable or volatile? I am sure you are in a position to tell me."

Carruthers and Palmer exchanged a glance. Then Carruthers, with his habitual grin, said, "I am Tampica's Prime Minister, Mr. Tibbett. You could hardly expect me to tell you that the political situation is rocky. So I don't know if you will believe me when I say that we are on a remarkably even keel. You can see that our people are prosperous." He paused. "Now, don't get me wrong. I have the greatest admiration for Sir Edward Ironmonger, but in all honesty I must point out that under his administration the island's economy was sluggish. Sluggish, if not stagnant. I fear his ideas are rather old-fashioned. Don't you agree, Joe?"

"Oh, undoubtedly." Palmer nodded, sadly. "A fine man, but a stick-in-the-mud." Once again, Henry was struck by the curious use of outdated English idiom. "However, our electors are no fools. They spoke their minds very clearly through the ballot boxes at the last election."

Carruthers took up the theme. "And here we are, Mr. Tibbett, a set of new brooms, and already sweeping clean."

Henry said, "I read somewhere that the Tampican economy was in a bad way."

Carruthers's smile did not falter. "Don't you believe it, Mr. Tibbett. Don't you believe it. Well"—he made a big gesture in the direction of Pirate's Cave—"you only have to look and see for yourself. Under Sir Edward, I admit, the economy was in poor shape. But now—"

"What about the crime rate?" Henry asked.

"Desmond Kelly is the man to tell you about that—you remember, our Commissioner of Police. You met him last night. However," added Carruthers, smugly, "I can tell you that we are very fortunate. Crime in Tampica is minimal. Unlike some other islands I could mention. That is one of the reasons that our tourist industry is thriving. Our visitors feel safe here."

"You certainly make your island sound most desirable." Henry drained his glass. "Just one more question. How about drugs?"

There was a tiny pause, and then Carruthers said, "Joe, I'm sure Mr. Tibbett would like another rum punch."

"Of course. Allow me." Palmer took Henry's glass and went over to the drinks table.

Carruthers said, "If I told you, Mr. Tibbett, that we have no drug problem whatsoever on this island, you would not believe me, and you would be right. Of course we have a problem. Can you point to a single nation in the world, let alone in the Caribbean, which does not? All I can say is that our problem is not serious. I am thankful to say that our schoolchildren and young people in general are not affected. Also, hard drugs are virtually unheard of. Our only trouble is that many of the older men regard marijuana smoking not as a crime but as a way of life, as part of their heritage. It is not easy to re-educate them. Ah, here comes Joe with your drink."

It was an excellent performance, smooth and convincing. In ordinary circumstances, Henry reflected, he would probably have been taken in. In any case, he believed that what the Prime Minister had said was largely true. The drugs from which Tampicans made their fortunes were not consumed on the island. He began to feel distinctly depressed about the task that Lucy and Sir Edward had set him. Chester Carruthers was certainly not the man to indulge in indiscreet interviews or to overlook hidden tape recorders.

Aloud, Henry said, "Well, that's a very frank and fair statement, Mr. Prime Minister. If everything is as you say, I would imagine that Tampica would be a very interesting prospect for overseas investors."

"That is our hope," said Carruthers, with his unwavering smile.

Henry changed the subject. "I've been meaning to ask you something. Friends in London told me that there was a remarkable old lady living here—an Englishwoman with some sort of double-barreled name. Is she still alive?"

"Miss Pontefract-Deacon? Yes, she is still alive."

"I was wondering if my wife and I should pay her a visit. A sort of courtesy call."

For the first time, Chester Carruthers abandoned his smile and allowed his features to fall into a solemn expression. "I would not recommend it, Mr. Tibbett."

"You wouldn't?"

"No. For one thing, she lives on the other side of the mountain, at Sugar Mill Bay."

"But we're planning to hire a Jeep—"

"That is not my main objection, Mr. Tibbett." Carruthers sighed. "The truth of the matter is that you would very likely have a wasted journey. The lady is ninety years old, and I fear she has reached an advanced state of senility. Most of the time, she just sits staring out to sea, unaware of anything going on around her. At other moments, she appears to have

36

regained her wits—until one begins to talk to her. Then it becomes obvious that she is merely rambling. She suffers from bizarre delusions and comes out with every kind of nonsense." Carruthers gave a little laugh. "How do I know this? I will tell you. Miss Lucy was indeed a great personage on this island when she was younger. Many of us Tampicans owe a great deal to her, and love her. So people like myself feel in duty bound to visit her now and then. But it is not a happy experience, Mr. Tibbett. Not a happy experience."

"Oh, well," said Henry. "We'll probably do the drive over the mountain, anyway. But I'm very grateful to you for telling me this, Mr. Carruthers. Of course, my English friends have not seen her for many years, and obviously don't know—"

"Exactly." Carruthers cheered up again. "You have touched on a point which I wished to mention. Once, this island was part of the British Empire, and attracted a lot of British tourists. Now our visitors are almost all American. However, the U.K. and European markets are a growing source of tourism, and if some enterprising person—in London, let us say—were to organize charter flights to overcome the high cost of transatlantic travel, we could put together very interesting package holidays at Barracuda Bay and even Pirate's Cave. You see how it is, Mr. Tibbett? There are opportunities everywhere, just crying out for men of vision and foresight to invest their capital."

At the other end of the terrace, Emmalinda Palmer had gone indoors to organize lunch, and Emmy was finding Carmelita somewhat hard going. Whereas the night before she had been quick-smiling and apparently eager to talk, today her beautiful beige face was glum. She leaned on the parapet and gazed moodily into the distance.

Emmy said, brightly, "Mr. Palmer took us on a wonderful

tour of the island this morning, Mrs. Carruthers." No response. Emmy plowed on. "I didn't like to suggest it, because I thought the men wouldn't be interested, but one day I'd love to visit one of the day-care centers you were telling me about."

Carmelita turned and looked vaguely at Emmy. "What? What were you saying?"

"Day-care nurseries for preschool children of working mothers," said Emmy, very distinctly.

Carmelita did not answer, but turned away again. On the sea below the house, a little sailboat with a brightly striped spinnaker was running before the wind. Inconsequentially, Carmelita said, "That's one of Chester's sailboats. One of his kids must have taken it out."

"I didn't know you had children," said Emmy. "That must make your day-care work very—"

"I don't have children," said Carmelita, shortly. Then, "I like to sail. You like to sail?"

"I'm afraid I don't know anything about boats." Emmy had no intention of getting involved in a conversation about sailing. She was determined to establish her do-gooder image. "I was talking about these day-care centers—"

"Oh, yes." Carmelita opened her handbag—a very fine leather one by Gucci, as Emmy could not help noticing—and pulled out a handkerchief. She buried her face in it and blew her nose. A little unsteadily, she said, "I'm sorry. Caught a cold. Shouldn't really have come . . ."

But was it a cold, Emmy wondered, or was Carmelita hiding tears? Emmy glanced down the terrace at the implacably smiling Chester Carruthers. It was impossible to tell what went on behind that smile, but Emmy shivered slightly and felt glad that she was not married to him. She said, sympathetically, "I'm so sorry. It's always worse to catch cold in a sunny climate than it is in foggy old London."

"London . . ." Carmelita blew her nose again, and once more turned to watch the little sailboat. Emmy was extremely relieved when Emmalinda Palmer came billowing out of the house in her magnificent yellow-and-green batik caftan, booming merrily that lunch was ready.

Lunch was a buffet meal of mixed American and West Indian dishes, presided over by a bevy of polite, giggly girls whom Emmy gathered were not servants, but junior members of the family. The Tibbetts sampled goat water (delicious goat-meat stew), rice and pigeon peas, black bean soup and conch fritters, as well as more conventional salads. To end up with, there was homemade carrot cake and bananas flambéed in rum. As a graceful gesture to their overseas visitors, the Palmers had produced a couple of bottles of very sweet, warm white wine, but the Tampicans carried on drinking rum throughout the meal, and after a sip of the wine, the Tibbetts joined them.

When it was all over, and Emmy said that they really must get back to the hotel, Joe Palmer said, "I trust you'll forgive me, Mrs. Tibbett, but Chester and I have business to do. For us, this is supposed to be a working lunch. I'll get my driver to take you back to Pirate's Cave."

In the car, Henry and Emmy rode in silence. It was not until they were in the privacy of their own cottage that Henry said, "Well, that was certainly an interesting experience."

"Did you get anywhere?" Emmy asked.

"Yes and no. Tampica is obviously not short of money, and yet Carruthers is frantically trying to raise funds. That makes me think he may be keen to get out of the drug trade."

"Some hope," Emmy remarked.

39

"I agree," said Henry. "But he's not a stupid man. However, the easiest thing to concentrate on for the moment is this boat."

"What boat?"

"Didn't you see her? A big motor cruiser with a dark blue hull. I noticed her coming in to Frigate Bay—which must have been why Palmer hustled us away so fast. When I asked later, he claimed not to have seen the boat. Then, at lunchtime, she was hanging round off the beach here. Palmer said she belongs to some Americans."

"You think she's being used for drug running?"

"Almost certainly." Henry had taken off his shirt and was rummaging in the closet for his swimming trunks. "But if Lucy's right, she'll be just one of a whole fleet of boats, and light planes, too. I'm inclined to think there's more to it than that. Oh, I didn't tell you."

"Tell me what?"

"I asked Carruthers very discreetly about Lucy—said I didn't know her, but had been told about her, and suggested we might visit her. That rattled him, I can tell you. He told me that she's senile—completely gaga most of the time, and quite irrational at others."

"In other words—if we did go and see her, and she started on about drugs on the island, we'd be supposed to think there wasn't a word of truth in it."

"Exactly. Now, let's go and have a swim. And afterward—I think we'll visit Lucy, just the same."

4

Formalities concerning the hiring of a self-drive Jeep for a week were reduced to a minimum for guests at Pirate's Cave. All that was required was a sum of money—three times as much as Henry remembered from his previous visit—to obtain a small piece of pink paper that represented a local driving license, valid for one month. By four o'clock the Tibbetts were on their way over the mountain to Sugar Mill Bay.

The views from the top of the winding road were as breathtaking as they remembered, panoramas of crinkling sapphire sea breaking in feathers of white spray over gray rocks and crawling lazily up creamy crescents of coral sand. The road, however, was very different. The boulder-strewn dirt track of six years before was now a serpentine ribbon of dirty white concrete, and at the most precipitous points a stout stone wall stood between the Jeep and a possible plunge onto the beach a thousand feet below.

"It spoils the view" was Emmy's verdict.

Henry laughed. "Remember how scared you were the first time we did this drive, with an unpaved road and no parapet at all?"

"Oh, well—the first time, maybe. But after that—"

Behind them, a loud motor horn tooted impatiently. They

41

had reached the summit and were on a comparatively straight stretch of road—one of the few places where vehicles could pass. In his mirror, Henry saw a big black American car tailgating him. As the horn sounded again, fretfully, Henry pulled the Jeep well onto the side of the road, and the other car flashed past at dangerous speed. All that Henry could see was a blur of black window glass, which prevented him from identifying the driver.

Emmy said, "There goes an accident just waiting to happen. Did you see who it was?"

"Not a hope."

"Henry, do you think we're being followed?"

"We're certainly not being followed now."

"You know what I mean."

"It's possible, but I really don't care much. I told Carruthers that we were planning to drive over the mountain anyhow. Ah, look—there's Sugar Mill Bay."

Ahead of them, the road snaked steeply down to the small settlement of gaudily painted cottages far below; and beyond the village, almost on the beach, they could see the conical gray shape of the ruined sugar mill that gave the place its name. Close to the mill, but hidden now by coconut palms, they knew they would find the graceful white house, with its big old-fashioned veranda and intricately carved trellises, which for nearly a century had been Lucy Pontefract-Deacon's home.

Driving through the little village, Emmy kept a sharp lookout for the black car, but there was no sign of it. Since there was only one road, and the car had certainly not returned, it must be parked out of sight behind one of the houses, unless it was actually at Lucy's place. But there was no sign of it in the driveway, as Henry swung the Jeep through the ever open gates of Sugar Mill House.

As they climbed out, Henry said, "I don't want to be melodramatic, but it's just possible we're being watched—so play it as though we haven't met Lucy before."

Emmy nodded, and they climbed the steps to the veranda. The white-painted louvered doors leading to the sitting room were closed, so Henry tapped them gently and called out, "Miss Pontefract-Deacon! Anybody at home?"

After a moment, there was a scuffle of feet inside, and then the door was opened by a youth in a very neat white jacket, black trousers, and bare feet. Henry was relieved to see that he was not the same young man who had greeted them on their last visit. He remembered that Lucy's domestic staff always underwent a brisk turnover—not because she was an unpopular employer, but because once she had trained a boy to her impeccable standards, he found it easy to move on to more challenging work in the hotel industry. He remembered Lucy's remark about the reliability of the manager of Pirate's Cave, and speculated that years ago that distinguished gentleman had probably served his apprenticeship at Sugar Mill House.

The present incumbent, who looked about seventeen, said, "I will tell Miz Lucy you are here, sir. What name shall I say?"

"Tibbett. Mr. and Mrs. Tibbett."

"Yes, sir. Please come in and sit down. Just one moment.

It was cool and quiet in the living room, with its big wooden-bladed fan whirring softly and its louvers filtering the sunlight. Henry and Emmy sat down and waited.

It was nearly five minutes before the door from the living quarters opened and Lucy appeared, looking magnificent and very much at home in a long skirt of crinkly blue cotton and a loose, dark brown overshirt. Glancing back over her shoulder, she said, "I shan't need you for the moment,

Samuel, but please make three rum punches and bring them in a few minutes." Then she closed the door behind her, looked at the Tibbetts with unusual solemnity, and said, "Is this wise?"

"I think so," Henry said. He held out his hands, which Lucy took with a big smile. "I told Carruthers we had heard your name from English friends, and intended to pay a courtesy call."

"Good for you." Lucy beamed. "What did he say?"

It was Emmy who answered. "He told Henry you were senile and strongly advised him not to come here."

Lucy laughed with genuine amusement. "The best he could do on the spur of the moment, I suppose." She sat down. "Well, now, tell me what's happening. But not in front of Samuel. Not that I don't trust him—but these days one can't be too careful."

Henry said, "Sir Edward is being splendid. He managed to introduce us to Carruthers, Palmer, and Kelly with no fuss. He and I, you see, were distant acquaintances from Washington days—and I would have you remember, Lucy, that I am an extremely wealthy retired businessman with funds to invest—"

"Oh, Henry," Lucy interrupted, "I know all this. It was my idea. Get on."

"Well, this morning we were taken on a tour of the island, and various investment possibilities were pointed out. Did I say pointed out? We had our noses rubbed in them. Afterwards, a delightful lunch at the Palmer house."

"So why are you here?" Lucy demanded.

At that moment, Samuel appeared with the drinks.

Lucy said smoothly, "—or rather, why you are here. Thank you, Samuel. Just put the tray down on the table." She glanced at her watch. "Five o'clock. Time you were off home, Samuel."

"If you need me to stay, Miz Lucy—"

"No, no. I can manage. You run along."

When Samuel had gone, Lucy continued. "You've met Brinkman?"

Henry shook his head. "Only to exchange one word with. He seems to spend all his time parasailing."

"Oh, these new crazes." Lucy dismissed the sport with a gesture. "Of course, it's a good way of remaining incommunicado. One is vulnerable on a beach. However—go on."

Henry leaned forward. "I'm interested in a boat. I think you may be able to help me."

"To hire one, you mean? Here, take your drink. What do you want with a boat, Henry?"

Henry shook his head. "Not to hire. I mean, I'm interested in a particular boat which we've seen around twice today. I don't know her name, but she's a big motor cruiser with a dark blue hull, and Carruthers says she belongs to some Americans."

Lucy laughed. "That could be a description of about a hundred boats in Tampican waters."

"Oh, dear," said Henry. "I can see I'll have to get more details. But—you know so much of what happens here, Lucy. Does it suggest any particular boat to you?"

"Of course it does. It sounds to me like *Bellissima*, which belongs to a rather shady character called De Marco."

"Italian?"

"American Italian," Lucy corrected. Her eyes twinkled. "Of course, it's impossible not to make the connection. And I'll tell you something I was saving up as a *bonne bouche*. Thomas Brinkman didn't arrive here by air, like most people, but aboard *Bellissima*. So I was going to ask you to find out all you could about the boat. Apparently, Brinkman's story is that he's a bad sailor, got fed up with cruising, and decided to put up in a comfortable hotel. So he had his friends drop him off in Tampica Harbour. But *Bellissima* didn't continue her cruise down-island. As you say, she's still hanging around in these waters."

"To the embarrassment," Henry remarked, "of Palmer and Carruthers. I told Emmy I thought she might be more than an ordinary drug runner." He paused. "Why didn't you tell me in London about Brinkman and *Bellissima*?"

"Because I didn't know then. Otherwise, of course I would have."

"And Sir Edward didn't mention it when we talked to him yesterday." Emmy sounded puzzled.

"I doubt," said Lucy, "if Eddie knows yet. The fact is that Samuel's girlfriend is an immigration officer. She happened to mention to him that Brinkman had arrived on *Bellissima* and jumped ship because of seasickness, and Samuel passed it on to me, quite innocently, yesterday afternoon. I wasn't really surprised, because I'd been having my doubts about De Marco."

"You know him?" Henry asked.

"Not really. What happened was that *Bellissima* dropped anchor here in the bay at lunchtime yesterday. De Marco came ashore asking for provisions, ice, and water. If he'd sailed around Tampica before, he'd have known that all you can get here is water, and mighty little of that. However, the local people did their best to help and sent him to me. He introduced himself, which is how I know his name. I gave him a bag of ice cubes, a couple of tins of food, and some advice." A pause. "I didn't like him."

Henry suppressed a smile. "Why, Lucy?"

"He wore what I can only describe as a yachting outfit," said Lucy, with deep distaste. "White trousers and a blazer, if you please. And a peaked cap."

"A sign of respect?" Emmy suggested.

Lucy snorted. "If he'd been an Englishman, he'd have known better. He was also too inquisitive."

"What do you mean by that?" Henry asked.

"I had the distinct impression that he was trying to pump me. Asking questions about secluded anchorages and deserted bays and so forth. And anyway, he had no need to look for provisions here. With a boat like *Bellissima*, he could be in Tampica Harbour within the hour."

"You didn't alert Sir Edward?"

"No, Henry, I didn't. Until Samuel told me about Brinkman's connection with the boat, it didn't seem important. Of course, Samuel saw her in the bay, and that's what led him to mention what his girlfriend had said. Since then, I've had no chance to talk to Eddie. I explained to you that it's not safe to use the telephone. And I certainly don't go visiting at Government House."

"So how do you keep in touch?"

"Eddie drives over about once a week. In fact, I was rather expecting him this afternoon."

Emmy said, "Not in a big black American car with dark windows?"

"Yes."

"Then I think he'll be here soon," said Henry. "Unless he decides to wait until we leave."

"What do you mean?"

"I mean, Lucy, that we were passed by just such a car on the way over. Of course, we couldn't see who was driving, but

47

he must have seen us. He's probably very angry with us. I think we'd better go at once. He's obviously waiting somewhere in the village until the coast is clear."

"Oh, dear." Lucy made a face, but did not sound unduly alarmed. "You picked a bad moment, didn't you? But I'm glad I've been able to tell you about *Bellissima*."

"You've set us one hell of a job, Lucy." Henry sounded depressed. "Any meetings will obviously be held on board the boat."

"I thought you two were sailors."

"That doesn't mean we can hide under the bunk of a motor cruiser with a tape recorder."

"Well, I'm sure you'll think of something." Lucy was soothing. She stood up. "Now you'd better go. Don't come here again."

"Can we get a message to you?" Henry asked.

Lucy considered. Then her face cleared. "Of course. Through Patrick."

"Who's Patrick?"

"The Manager of Pirate's Cave. I told you—I can trust him. If you give him a letter, he'll get it to me."

"I'm not keen on putting things in writing," Henry objected.

Lucy looked at him quizzically. "I think you will find that plain speech is just as dangerous on Tampica these days. Now, be off with you."

Henry stopped the Jeep at the high vantage point on the mountain that overlooked Sugar Mill Bay. The light was beginning to fade as the sun went down in a magnificent explosion of orange, green, and red beyond the western sea; but Henry could just see the shape of a big black car turning into the gates of Sugar Mill House.

By the time the Tibbetts arrived back at Pirate's Cave, the swift tropical twilight had deepened enough for the twinkling mushroom lights on the paths to come on, like glow-worms. From several of the guest cottages, pools of orange light spilled out into the cool silver of the evening—and one of these, Henry was interested to notice, was that of their next-door neighbor, Mr. Thomas Brinkman.

As they approached the cottage from the back, Henry said quietly, "If he's on his balcony, we'll try to get acquainted."

Emmy nodded. They rounded the building, to see that Brinkman was, indeed, sitting on the balcony outside his suite. He wore shorts and a T-shirt inscribed PARASAILORS DO IT HIGHER. His feet were propped up on the rattan table in front of him, which also held a half-full glass of reddish liquid.

Henry waved cheerfully. "You must be Mr. Brinkman!"

"Sure." The other's voice was slow, with a southern drawl.

"We're Henry and Emmy Tibbett. We're in the suite next door."

"Glad to know you folks." Brinkman did not get up, but he removed his feet from the table. "You from England?"

"Yes. Escaping the foul weather over there."

Emmy said, "We've been watching you parasailing, Mr. Brinkman. It must be terribly difficult and exciting."

Brinkman shook his head slowly. "Nothing to it. It's the guy in the boat who does all the work."

"But surely it's dangerous?" Emmy persisted.

"Only if the boatman doesn't know his job. And this hotel has the best. Young fellow, name of Dolphin."

"Dolphin! What an odd name."

"Oh, that's not his real name." Brinkman was still smiling.

"Round here, seems everybody has a nickname. I guess he's called Dolphin because he swims like one. You folks care for a rum punch?"

"That's very kind of you," said Henry. "We certainly would."

So the Tibbetts dropped into two vacant chairs, while Thomas Brinkman heaved himself out of his and went to his refrigerator inside the cottage. He emerged a few moments later with two brimming glasses.

"Your good health, Mr. . . . er . . ."

"Tibbett," said Henry.

"But please call us Henry and Emmy," Emmy put in.

"Your good health, Emmy . . . Henry . . ." They all drank. "My name's Tom. So—how have you been spending your time since you got here?"

Henry said, "We had a bit of a tour of the island this morning. Mr. Palmer took us—the Finance Minister."

"My, my." Brinkman sounded lazy and uninterested. "You folks sure do move in high society."

Emmy was quick to correct this. "No, not really. It just so happens that we met Sir Edward Ironmonger very briefly in Washington some years ago, when Henry was there on business. I believe you know him, too. We heard him greeting you in the dining room last night."

Brinkman looked displeased. "We have been introduced. But, frankly, I'm trying to avoid getting dragged into local affairs. I'm on vacation."

Henry smiled, a little ruefully. "I know what you mean. I daresay you've had the treatment, too."

"Treatment?"

"Trying to get you to invest in the island," Henry explained.

Brinkman shrugged. "Oh, that. Yeah. I let them know right away there was nothing doing."

"But . . ." Henry, cradling his glass, appeared to hesitate. "Don't you think there might be something in it? I mean, Tampica seems to be a fast-growing economy, with lots of potential and no serious problems of crime or drugs. . . ."

"Look, Henry," said Brinkman, "I'm on vacation, like I said. What you do with your money—that's your funeral. You needn't think I'm about to start giving you advice."

"No, no, of course not," said Henry hastily. There was a pause. Then Henry went on, on a different note. "Well, this afternoon we got away from politics. We hired a Jeep and drove over the mountain."

"Over the mountain?" Brinkman closed his eyes as he leaned back in his chair. "Why?"

"To see the view from the top, mainly," said Emmy. "It's spectacular, isn't it?"

Brinkman grunted assent. Henry said, "We should have turned round and come back down again, but we decided to go on and explore the village. Waste of time. Nothing there. We ended up driving into somebody's garden by mistake. Quite a biggish house. I don't think the owner can have been there. A rather superior sort of black butler came and chucked us out—very politely, of course. I wonder who lives there."

"No idea," said Brinkman shortly. "Never been over there myself."

"You haven't missed anything." Henry assured him. He looked at his watch. "Come on, darling. Drink up. We must go and change for dinner." The Tibbetts finished their drinks and stood up. "Many thanks for the punch, Tom. Shall we see you later?"

Brinkman shook his head. "Doubt it. Thought I'd go into town for a drink. Probably stay and grab a bite somewhere. This place is comfortable enough, but mealtimes have a touch more class than I need on vacation, to be honest."

"It is a bit overpowering," Henry agreed. "When we've been here a bit longer, I daresay we'll start exploring Tampica's seamy side."

Brinkman gave him the sort of look that this remark richly deserved. He mumbled, "Be seein' ya," picked up the empty glasses, and ambled into the cottage.

Back in their own quarters, Emmy said, "I wonder what he made of us?"

Henry grinned. "I hope," he said, "that we came across as rich and stupid, as well as conventional and snobbish. But you never can tell."

5

he first thing that Henry noticed next morning when he went out onto the veranda to savor the cool of the sunrise was *Bellissima*. The motor cruiser was riding at anchor in the bay of Pirate's Cave, where she must have arrived in the small hours, for there had been no sign of her when the Tibbetts went to bed at midnight. A sturdy motor dinghy of the Boston whaler type bobbed astern of her.

Henry nipped back into the cottage, where Emmy was still sleeping, to get his binoculars. Through them he could see every detail of the yacht. Her cabin doors were closed, but several hatches on deck were propped open to ventilate the accommodation inside. The large forehatch was wide open, and beside it sat a crew member, cross-legged, doing something intricate with a length of rope: a young white man in neat white shorts and a T-shirt with M/V BELLISSIMA stenciled on it in navy blue.

After a few minutes, evidently satisfied with his rope job, the young man got to his feet, went astern, and jumped lightly into the dinghy. In a matter of seconds he had cast off, started the outboard motor, and was headed for the hotel's landing stage. Running at minimum speed, the engine purred almost silently, and the whaler made scarcely a ripple in the quiet water. Henry ran back into the cottage, slipped into shorts and a shirt, and made his unobtrusive way through the shrubs and palm trees toward the jetty.

By the time he got close to the landing stage, the dinghy was tied up and the young crewman was ashore making his way up across the lawn toward the reception area of the hotel. There were very few people about. On the beach, three men with rakes and shoulder packs of insecticide were spraying, tidying, and smoothing the sand, so that the earliest of the hotel guests would find it impeccable and bug-free. A gardener was languidly raking up colorful petals of fallen bougainvillea and snipping off dead hibiscus heads—yesterday's brilliant flowers, for the hibiscus blooms and dies in a day. Another gardener was making his way across the lawns, squatting down at intervals to turn on sprinklers that sent out huge umbrellas of fine spray to keep the cropped grass green. Otherwise, there was nobody around. It was too early for the staff of the kitchen or the Reception Desk, and although Henry knew that security guards would be on patrol, their presence was kept tactfully unobtrusive.

Henry glanced at his watch. Just after six. In the short time since he had first noticed *Bellissima*, the sky had lightened enough to allow the beach and garden workers to go about their business, and every minute brought full daylight nearer. He decided that it would not be an impossible hour for an enthusiastic jogger to be out, and consequently he began to jog, his path leading him toward the young sailor as he climbed the slope from the jetty.

As he came level with the young man, Henry waved cheerfully, then, panting slightly as if glad of an excuse to stop, he said, "Good morning! Can I help you? Nobody much about yet, I'm afraid."

"Oh—good morning. No thanks. Just leaving a note in Reception."

"Won't be anyone there before half-past seven, you know. All locked up."

"That's okay. Thanks all the same."

Henry waved again, in the manner of one who has done all he can, and set off again. As soon as his jogging took him behind a protective screen of shrubbery, he stopped and turned around. The young American—well-bred and from the northeastern seaboard by his voice—had reached the Reception Desk. As Henry had pointed out, it was closed and securely protected by a padlocked iron grille. Behind it were the rows of pigeonholes waiting for guests' mail or messages, and beyond them the door to the room where strongboxes were kept.

At the desk, the American stopped and pulled a piece of paper from his pocket. He started trying to push it through under the iron grille, where it joined the desktop. This proved impossible, for the grille was tight-fitting. He then tried to shove the paper through the grating, but the grille was backed by fine wire mesh. Finally, he decided to shove the message through at the side, where the grille joined the stonework of the building. This was easier, as the stonework was uneven, and did not provide a tight seal.

Slowly, he wriggled the folded paper through until only a fraction of it protruded on the outside. At this point, it apparently occurred to him that if he pushed it all the way through it would fall onto the end of the semicircular desk, which at that point was very narrow, and might easily end up on the ground and be overlooked. At any rate, for whatever reason, the young sailor decided to leave it as it was—surely very obvious to the first person who came on duty and unlocked the grille. His mission accomplished, he went off down the lawn to the jetty, whistling to himself.

It was not until the motorboat was on its way, and well out

of sight of the reception area, that Henry emerged from his hiding place and continued his jogging toward the desk.

The gardener who was tidying the leaves gave him a brief look, but showed no special interest—joggers were clearly not unusual, and the sensible ones chose the cool of the morning to take their exercise. Nevertheless, Henry reckoned that it would cause remark, at the least, if he appeared to be raiding the desk. So he put on what was probably an unnecessary charade of stopping abruptly and rubbing his ankle, as if he might have twisted it. He was close to the desk and limped a couple of paces up to it so that he could lean against it for support. This gave him ample opportunity to whisk the scrap of paper from its lodging.

It was typewritten and had no name on the outside fold, only a number. The number of Brinkman's cottage. The edges of the folded paper were stuck together with transparent tape, but it was easy to bend the paper into a tube. Squinting up it, Henry read: "This evening, 5:30, usual place."

Quickly, he replaced the paper. He went through the motions of trying out his ankle, and then resumed his jogging—this time back to his own cottage.

Emmy was up and about, leaning on the balcony rail in her filmy Indian cotton housecoat. She was about to greet Henry when he put his finger to his lips. Surprised, she followed him into the cottage.

"Whatever—?" she began, but once again Henry silenced her with a warning gesture. He went into the bathroom, turned a tap full on, and beckoned her to join him.

"What's all the secrecy?" Emmy sounded amused.

"Sorry, darling. But Brinkman might have been able to hear anything you said outside, and even in here—well, I'm taking no chances. Running water is a pretty good way of masking speech."

"But what's it all about and where have you been, Henry?"

Henry grinned. "Out for an early morning jog. Did you see *Bellissima*?"

"The big motor cruiser? She was leaving just as you came back."

"I thought as much. Thank goodness I got up to look at the sunrise."

"What does that mean?"

Henry told her. Emmy said, "I see. Where's 'the usual place'?"

"I only wish I knew. It could be Frigate Bay—or it could be anywhere. I think I'll have to get in touch with Sir Edward."

"At the cloak-and-dagger number?"

"Of course. We obviously can't call from here. Get dressed, and after breakfast we'll drive into town and find a call box."

There was no sign of Tom Brinkman in the dining room, but by the time the Tibbetts had returned to their cottage and prepared for their expedition into Tampica Harbour, the familiar parachute was drifting lazily between sea and sky over the bay. But Brinkman must have paid a visit, however brief, to the main hotel complex, because Henry noticed on his way to breakfast that the folded note was in Brinkman's pigeonhole, and on his way back it was gone.

There was a row of public telephone booths outside the post office in Tampica Harbour. Henry chose the most remote, set Emmy as a lookout, and dialed the number Ironmonger had given him.

The phone rang three times, and then a soft, feminine, and very West Indian voice answered. "Melinda's Market. Melinda Murphy here. Can I help you?"

"Oh." Henry was taken aback. "I'm afraid I must have the wrong number."

"This is 59321," replied the voice, giving the number Henry had dialed. "Who did you wish to speak with?"

"I'm trying to get hold of Edward," said Henry.

"Oh, yes?" The voice was unsurprised. "Who is speaking, please?"

"Scott."

"Just one moment, please." A pause, during which Henry could hear in the background a bustle of sound that might indeed have come from a store. Then the voice was back. "Yes, Mr. Scott. If you will give me your number, Edward will call you back as soon as he can."

"I'm speaking from a call box. Tell him to call me at"—Henry hesitated, then came up with a brainwave—"at Barney's bar in about half an hour. It'll be open then, won't it?"

"Surely. Barney opens for breakfast."

"Good. So tell him that. Okay?"

"Okay, Mr. Scott."

"Many thanks." Henry hung up.

Outside, Emmy was pretending to read the excessively dull notices on the post office door. She said, "Did you get through?"

"Yes. But he has to call me back. I said we'd be at Barney's, so let's get down there. Anything suspicious here?"

Emmy laughed. "How could there be? Just a few honest citizens and tourists posting letters and buying stamps. How clever of you to think of Barney's. It'll be fun to see it again."

When the Tibbetts had first visited Tampica, Barney's Bar and Garage had been a collection of shacks on the waterfront. The garage had consisted of one battered gasoline pump and a ramshackle workshop, roofed but without walls. The bar had been a little concrete house with rickety metal tables and scuffed wooden chairs. Hens and goats had roamed freely around the dusty compound, and Barney himself—a genial giant of a man—had presided with great good humor over both establishments. On a more recent flying visit, Henry and Emmy had seen big changes— a modern, well-equipped garage and a restaurant sporting a terrace with tables shaded by big striped umbrellas. But Barney himself had still been there, as reassuring as ever, although it was clear that he had pretty well handed the restaurant over to a manager, and was concentrating on the garage business.

Now, the restaurant had expanded yet again into a most imposing establishment, with a huge marble terrace overlooking the sea, where tourists sat at white-painted wrought-iron tables between potted palms and tubs of bougainvillea—the late risers still finishing breakfast, the early drinkers already starting on Bloody Marys. Henry and Emmy sat down and ordered coffee. Then Henry said to the waiter, "Oh, by the way, I'm expecting a phone call. The name's Scott. You'll let me know when it comes through?"

"No problem, sir." White teeth flashed, and the waiter was gone. The Tibbetts had not finished their first cup of coffee when he was back.

"The telephone's through here, sir. Just follow me."

"Yes, Scott. What is it?" Sir Edward's rich voice was unmistakable.

"I'd like to see you as soon as possible," said Henry. "This is urgent."

"Wait outside Barney's. I'll pick you up in ten minutes."

Sir Edward Ironmonger did not keep Caribbean time. It was actually nine and a half minutes later that a black car with tinted windows pulled up beside the Tibbetts, who were ostensibly window-shopping at a boutique next door to the restaurant.

The back door opened and they climbed in. Sir Edward was alone, driving himself. The car pulled away at once and turned in the direction of Pirate's Cave.

"Well, Henry, what is it?"

"We need to talk, Sir Edward. Somewhere private."

"Very well."

The car turned off the main road and down a winding lane leading to the sea. After only a few yards, Ironmonger left the track and parked the car in the shelter of a grove of coconut palms.

The beach that lay ahead would have prompted the development of an instant resort hotel in most countries, but by Tampican standards it was mediocre: only a narrow strip of sand and no dramatic rocks to break the flat blue seascape. Consequently, it was deserted.

Sir Edward switched off the engine and said, "We should be private here. But I can't stay long. Be quick, please."

Henry said, "There's to be a rendezvous this evening on board a boat called *Bellissima*."

"A rendezvous? Between whom?"

"Brinkman for one. And the owner of the boat, I assume. With any luck, Carruthers and/or the others in the Tampican connection will be there too."

Sir Edward frowned. "Where is this meeting to take place?"

"I wish I knew, sir. I managed to intercept the message left for Brinkman this morning, but it just said 'the usual place.' "

"Wait a minute." Ironmonger was suddenly alert. "The *Bellissima*, you said? De Marco's boat?"

"That's right. I suppose Lucy told you—"

"That makes things much easier. I shall invite De Marco and his crew to lunch with me at Pirate's Cave."

"You know him, Sir Edward?" Emmy asked.

"Not as yet, Mrs. Tibbett. But Carruthers and Palmer have been very keen for me to make contact with him—offer him some entertainment and show him the island. He has been described to me as a big potential investor."

"With truth, I should say," said Henry dryly.

"But if he's involved in drug running, why should they want you to meet him?" Emmy was puzzled.

Ironmonger smiled. "I am respectable," he said. "I am also the Governor-General. I imagine that I am to lend respectability to this De Marco, and he is to lend a whiff of a criminal connection to me, which might come in useful." He lit a cigar. "Well, Chester shall have his wish. What time is this meeting scheduled?"

"Half past five."

"Very satisfactory. My luncheon party will be at one."

Emmy began to say, "I don't see what—" at the same moment that Henry said, "But how will you—?" Their remarks collided in midair.

Ironmonger grinned and puffed his cigar. "I will answer you both," he said. "First of all—how shall I make contact with De Marco? By radio, naturally. All boats in these waters listen out on an allocated channel, and I have the necessary equipment at Government House. Secondly, what good will it do? Very simple. It will mean that *Bellissima* is anchored off Pirate's Cave and left unattended for some time." He turned to Henry. "I presume that you have some sort of tape recorder with you?"

"Of course. A small battery-run machine, activated by the human voice."

"Good. How you get it on board and installed is your affair. It will also be up to you to remove it again. Meanwhile, let us hope that it will provide us with exactly the evidence we need." He paused, then added, "I wonder what is the direct connection with *Bellissima*? Joe Palmer told me that she arrived with quite a party of people aboard, but that the guests had left her in Tampica, and De Marco was cruising on his own, with just one young crewman."

Emmy said, "Brinkman arrived here aboard her, Sir Edward. Lucy must have told you."

"Lucy?" Ironmonger frowned. "No. But I haven't seen Lucy for some time, and you know we don't speak of these things on the telephone."

"But—we saw you visiting her yesterday," Emmy protested. "In this car."

Sir Edward shook his head. "Not me," he said. "I had hoped to drive over, but I couldn't get away."

"Then who could it have been?" Henry wandered. "We were passed on the mountain by a car just like this one, and later we saw it turn into Lucy's driveway."

"Oh, there are quite a few of these cars on the island." Sir Edward did not sound concerned. "All government departments have them. And Lucy is still a great figure on Tampica, you know. Plenty of people visit her." He glanced at his watch. "Now I must go and organize my lunch party. I'll leave you in Tampica Harbour. When you see *Bellissima* dropping anchor and her crew coming ashore, you'll know everything is in order. If things go wrong, I'll get a message to you." He held out his hand. "Good luck, Henry."

"Thank you, sir."

"My name is Eddie, as you very well know. I wish you'd use it." The Governor-General beamed, and started the engine.

Back in the cottage at Pirate's Cave, Henry opened his

camera case—quite a large and elaborate affair—and took out a slim, black rectangular item that could have been a light meter. The camera case, being full of such small devices, made a good hiding place for the miniature tape recorder. As a precaution, however, Henry had fixed a hair-thin black thread across the opening of the pocket that held the recorder, and he was pleased to find it still in place.

He put the recorder on top of the refrigerator, then walked to the middle of the room, several yards away, and said, "Darling, throw me my blue bathing trunks, will you?"

"Okay. Here they come." Emmy, who was in the bathroom, tossed the bathing trunks into the living room.

"Thanks, love."

Henry went over to the refrigerator, picked up the recorder, and took it into the bathroom. He turned a tap full on, then opened the little flat box and made some adjustments. Almost at once, his voice—not loud but perfectly clear—played back to him. Even Emmy's voice from the bathroom, though faint, was audible. Satisfied, Henry wiped the tape clean and reset the machine. Then it went into a waterproof oilskin case, and Henry changed into the blue bathing trunks.

Emmy was already in her swimsuit, sipping rum punch on the balcony. Henry joined her. When they had finished their drinks, they picked up their beach towels and strolled down to the sea. The recorder fitted snugly into the small pocket with which the manufacturer, for some strange reason, had equipped Henry's swimming trunks. At the beach they set up a couple of reclining chairs under a palm-frond bohia and settled down for a morning's basking.

Bellissima arrived precisely at noon, just as many of the sunbathers were beginning to collect their belongings and straggle up toward the dining room for lunch. The same young man whom Henry had seen earlier was up on the bows, ready to drop the anchor; at the wheel stood a tall, very dark man, naked but for miniscule red trunks. He maneuvered the boat to a precise and skillful stop in the center of the bay: down went the anchor, and the purr of the engine stopped. Then the helmsman disappeared down the companionway.

Gazing up at the sky, Emmy said, "I wonder where Tom Brinkman is today." For once, the gaudy parachute lay neatly packed on the raft, while the boatman and his three assistants swam lazily around, waiting for customers.

"Lunching in town, I expect," Henry said. It would be understandable that Brinkman would want to keep out of the way while Sir Edward entertained De Marco. But how could he have known about the lunch party? Surely he couldn't have a radio receiver and transmitter? And yet—why not? The fact that his own notification of the rendezvous had arrived in the form of a note simply meant that such a message could obviously not be sent over the radio, where every boat and many hotels and private people in the area would hear it.

The beach was now emptying fast, and soon Henry and Emmy were alone except for a couple of sun-worshipers who had not moved their glistening young bodies all morning except to roll over to grill a different skin area; and a pair of stout elderly gentlemen in decorous Bermuda shorts, both of whom had fallen noisily asleep, and who would undoubtedly regret staying out so long in the sun, despite their floppy white linen hats.

Then the crew of *Bellissima* appeared on deck. The fair boy was wearing white shorts and a T-shirt, as he had earlier, but De Marco had changed into full yachting regalia—long white trousers, a white shirt with a silk scarf knotted at the neck, an immaculate navy blue blazer. Emmy remembered Lucy's description. The two men climbed down a ladder on the starboard side of the boat into the dinghy, and soon the outboard motor was bringing them gently alongside the landing stage.

Through half-closed eyes, Henry watched the men clamber ashore. While the young man moored the dinghy, De Marco straightened his shoulders and brushed down the sleeves of his blazer. Then, satisfied that he was sartorially perfect, he led the way up the grassy slope toward the dining room. Sir Edward's lunch party was about to begin.

Henry gave them five minutes, just in case of any snags. Then he sat up and said to Emmy, "Coming in for a dip?"

"Yes." Emmy stretched and got up from her beach bed. They walked down to the sea together.

At the edge of the water there were several plastic boards, lightweight and buoyant, which lazy bathers could use as floating mattresses to save themselves the exertion of swimming. Henry and Emmy took one each and waded out into waist-deep water, where they climbed onto their boards and, lying face down, began to paddle idly around the bay. The two couples on the beach took absolutely no notice of them. Nevertheless, Henry knew that they could be seen from the terrace of the hotel, so he took his time in maneuvering himself toward the anchored motorboat.

Fortunately, the prevailing breeze caused *Bellissima* to swing broadside on to the beach, so that her seaward side was hidden from any watchers ashore—and it was on this side that the boarding ladder hung. While Emmy drifted between *Bellissima* and the beach, Henry paddled himself around the stern of the boat and into the shelter of the seaward side. Once there, he slipped into the water, and wedged his raft under the ladder to stop it from floating away. Holding the lowest rung of the ladder with one hand, he treaded water, waiting.

Emmy's idle paddling on her plastic board was not as aimless as it appeared. She was able to keep an eye both on the beach and on the portion of the hotel terrace from which *Bellissima* was visible. Soon, the bronzed young couple roused themselves, collected their suntan lotions and towels, and made their way slowly up to the hotel. Only the two white and corpulent gentlemen slept on, breathing stertorously. Emmy decided that the moment had come. Quickly, she paddled herself around *Bellissima*'s stern and gave Henry a thumbs-up sign.

Henry was up the ladder, on board, and down the companionway in a couple of seconds flat. He found himself in a large and luxurious saloon, furnished with the usual bunk benches and fixed central table—the latter of brightly varnished wood, with fiddles to keep glasses and crockery from falling off in rough weather. He looked around quickly. Above and behind the benches there were varnished storage lockers, each with a couple of holes in its door, into which you inserted your fingers to release the snap closure. Henry opened one, revealing a couple of charts, some string, and an assortment of courtesy flags.

Henry slipped the little recorder in under the flags, closed the locker again, and was back in the water in a trice. He knew that his dripping body must have left some water on the cabin floor, but with the hatchway open it would dry off in minutes in the tropical sun. He retrieved his paddling board, and soon he and Emmy were back on the beach. The terrace was still deserted, the two old men soundly asleep.

"Although how I'm going to get it back again," Henry remarked to Emmy under the protective noise of his gushing shower in their cottage, "heaven alone knows."

Heaven knew—and so, very soon, did Henry.

6

ir Edward's luncheon party was still going on when
Henry and Emmy came into the dining area for their
own belated meal. The Governor-General had
brought along his Prime Minister and his Finance
Minister to complete the party, and there was a lot of laughter
and cigar smoke over coffee and liqueurs. It was obvious that
De Marco was being given the same treatment as had been
administered to Henry. The young crewman sat silently
between Palmer and Carruthers, looking awkward and out of
place.

The three Tampicans greeted the Tibbetts warmly, and Sir
Edward introduced them to his guests. "This is Mr. De
Marco—I expect you've noticed his cruiser in the bay. And
Randy Porter,who does the hard work on board." Ironmonger
beamed. "Mr. and Mrs. Tibbett," he explained, "are refugees
from the English weather. We met in Washington some years
ago, and I like to think that it may have been my description
of Tampica that influenced their choice of vacation."

De Marco pronounced himself delighted to meet Sir
Edward's English friends, and the boy, Randy, mumbled
something and gazed down into his coffee cup.

"Well, well," Sir Edward continued, "we mustn't keep you
from your lunch. Been working up an appetite on the beach,
I daresay."

67

Joseph Palmer said, "I wonder, Mr. Tibbett, if you've had time to think over—"

"Nothing like an energetic swim to make you enjoy your food," interposed Carruthers, with a brief warning look at his colleague. "A keen appetite makes the best sauce, as our French cousins tell us."

Henry and Emmy smiled, made a few polite remarks, and took themselves off to a far table—but not so far as to prevent them from hearing Palmer urging De Marco to come on a conducted tour of the island. De Marco, however, refused the offer courteously but firmly. He was sailing immediately after lunch, he explained, as he had arranged to pick up some friends on a neighboring island. Shortly after that the party broke up, with much shaking of hands and promises to repeat the occasion when *Bellissima* returned to Tampica, which De Marco assured his host would be within a few days.

When the party had dispersed—the Tampicans to their black limousines, the Americans back to *Bellissima*—Henry said, "Well, so far, so good. Now all we can do is wait."

Once the waiter had taken their orders and withdrawn, Emmy said, "I've been thinking."

"Oh? What about, in particular?"

"That big black car that passed us going over the mountain, and then went in to Lucy's place. Who could it have been?"

"Ironmonger explained that," Henry assured her. "All the government people have those cars, and many of them visit Sugar Mill House."

"All the same, I can't help worrying a bit, Henry. I mean, this government isn't exactly packed with Lucy's friends. And she is terribly isolated over there. I wonder if we should drive over and make sure she's all right."

"Not again." Henry was firm. "She warned us not to. But

68

she did say we could send a letter via the manager here. Patrick, she called him."

"I don't much fancy doing that." Emmy was dubious. "In any case, what would one say in a letter? 'Who was your visitor? Are you all right?' It all sounds so silly."

After lunch, however, back in the cottage, Henry took a sheet of the hotel's letterhead notepaper from the desk and began writing, while Emmy lay on the bed, reading. He looked over what he had written, signed it, and passed it to Emmy.

"How about that? Is it okay?"

Emmy took the paper and read:

Dear Miss Pontefract-Deacon,

We did enjoy visiting you yesterday and were delighted to find you so well. We'd very much like to see you again soon. Please let us know when you think we could come over without tiring you too much.

Ever,
Henry Tibbett

Emmy nodded. "That should do," she said. "Nothing compromising there."

"Right. I'll take it up to the desk and try to locate this Patrick character." Henry stood up. "It will certainly tell Lucy that we want to get in touch. No need for you to come, darling. Stay and read your book. I shan't be long."

As Henry crossed the lawn toward the Reception Desk, he was just in time to see *Bellissima* nosing her way out through the narrow channel in the reef, her powerful motors throbbing quietly. He paused and watched as she turned to port and rounded the headland. She was certainly heading in the direction of Frigate Bay, but that was hardly informative. By half past five she could be almost anywhere. Henry sighed, and went on up to the desk.

As he approached, he saw that there was a tall man behind the desk with the female receptionist. Their heads were together as they pored over some sort of ledger. The receptionist looked up, saw Henry, and said with a smile, "Ah, Mr. Tibbett. Can I help you?"

"I'm looking for the manager, as a matter of fact," said Henry.

The receptionist's smile deepened into a beam, as she indicated the man beside her. "Right here, Mr. Tibbett. This is Mr. Bishop."

Mr. Patrick Bishop was a good-looking man, probably in his fifties, maybe older. He could have been a very light-skinned black or deeply suntanned white man. His dark brown eyes gave no indication of race. He held out his hand.

"Delighted to meet you, Mr. Tibbett. I hope you are enjoying your stay with us."

"Very much," Henry assured him, "but I wondered if I could have a word—"

"Certainly, certainly. Come into my office. This way."

Patrick Bishop led the way through a door behind the desk, and Henry found himself in the administrative section of the hotel. Typewriters clicked, secretaries and accountants went about their business. Henry caught a glimpse through an open door of a big board covered with strips of variously colored paper, which was the hotel's reservation chart. Once in Bishop's office, however, all was quiet and serene, except for the almost inaudible hum of the overhead electric fan.

"Do sit down, Mr. Tibbett. I take it your business has to do with Miss Lucy."

"She told me that you could get a letter to her more

quickly than the regular mail." He took the letter out of his shirt pocket. "Can you be very kind and get this to Sugar Mill House for me?"

The manager smiled. "No problem about that, Mr. Tibbett. The trouble is, Miss Lucy isn't there."

"Isn't there?" Henry was taken aback.

"She's off-island," Bishop explained. "Samuel—her general factotum—telephoned me this morning."

"Where is she?"

"That I don't know, sir. She often visits the British Seawards—she has friends there."

"I don't understand this," said Henry. "When did she go?"

"Yesterday evening, apparently."

"Apparently?"

"Yes. Samuel doesn't live in, you see. He lives with his mother in the village. It seems that when he came to work this morning, he found the house empty and a note from Miss Lucy saying that she had gone off-island for a few days, and telling him to notify me."

"She was still there when Samuel left yesterday afternoon?" Henry did not mention that he had been there himself.

"Oh, yes. He knocks off at five. She'd have had plenty of time to catch a late plane—but more likely she took the boat."

"What boat is that?"

"Our new interisland ferry," said Bishop, with a touch of pride. "The *Island Princess*. She makes the overnight journey from Tampica to Antigua three times a week—first stop, the British Seawards. Quite comfortable, if you can get a cabin."

"But Lucy would have to get over the mountain to Tampica Harbour," Henry pointed out.

"No, no. The *Princess* makes a short stop at Sugar Mill Bay wharf. There are a couple of new hotels at that end of the island now. Yesterday, Monday, is the day for her first run of the week."

Henry hesitated. Then he said, "I suppose there's no doubt that she really wrote that note?"

"Who else could have written it? Anyhow, Samuel knows her writing well enough."

"Oh, well." Henry stood up. "I suppose there's nothing to be done. Sorry to have taken up your time. Will Lucy let you know when she comes home?"

"I'm sure of it, Mr. Tibbett." Bishop paused, and then added. "I wouldn't worry, sir. Miss Lucy knows what she's doing."

"I hope you're right," said Henry.

On his way out, Henry was hailed by the receptionist. "Oh, Mr. Tibbett, I've got an envelope for you."

"An envelope? A letter, do you mean?"

"Well—I'm not sure. It feels like there's something solid inside." She reached into the pigeonhole marked with the number of the Tibbetts' cottage. "Here you are."

It did, indeed, feel as though there was something solid inside: small and solid and flat and slim. The envelope, which was made of heavy and expensive paper, was embossed with the words YACHT BELLISSIMA.

"Thank you very much," said Henry.

Emmy looked up from her book as Henry came in.

"All under control?" she asked.

Henry sat down on the bed. "All out of control," he said. "Lucy's disappeared."

"Disappeared?"

"Went off-island, apparently of her own free will, after we left her yesterday evening. This morning Samuel found a note from her, giving no idea of her destination or when she'd be back, and telling him to inform Mr. Bishop. And what's worse—just look at this."

He tore open the envelope and took out his tape recorder. Emmy looked at it, wide-eyed.

"They found it!"

"I think they did more than find it." Henry sounded grim. He adjusted the controls and pressed a button. At once, De Marco's voice came through, loud and clear.

"Mr. Tibbett, I don't pretend to know who you are or what you imagine you are playing at. Frankly, I don't care. All I care about is that you should stop meddling in my business. You fell neatly into the little trap I set for you. There is, of course, no rendezvous. I shall be back in Tampica tomorrow, and for your own safety you would be wise to leave the island before then. I should be sorry if you or your wife had an accident of any sort. You will not be warned again."

The voice stopped. Henry and Emmy looked at each other. Then Emmy said, "What are you going to do?"

Henry switched off the recorder. "I'm certainly not leaving Tampica. But it might be a good idea if you did. You could go to the Seawards and stay with—"

"The only person I'm staying with is you," said Emmy firmly.

Henry stood up. "Damn Lucy for going off like that." Then, "Somebody must have tipped De Marco off about us. How could he possibly have known otherwise?"

Emmy nodded. "It seems like that. But surely neither Lucy nor Sir Edward—"

Slowly, Henry said, "The only other person who may have an idea who I am is Bishop. Lucy said she trusted him, but I'm not so sure. Come to think of it, I've only got his word for it that Lucy *is* off-island. And, as you remarked, who was in that black

73

limousine if Ironmonger wasn't? Come on, darling. I don't care what Lucy said, we're going to Sugar Mill Bay."

No big black cars passed the Tibbetts' Jeep as it made its way over the mountain. The only traffic was a handful of other rented Jeeps, driven by palpable tourists who stopped at every lay-by to photograph the views. Henry, however, had no time for scenery. He was driving as fast as safety consid-erations permitted, and was nearly at the summit when, rounding a hairpin bend, he found himself confronted by the back end of a very large, very elderly truck, precariously laden with cement building blocks. The weight of its cargo plus the gradient of the road had reduced the speed of this lumbering Gargantua to about five miles an hour, and there was no hope of overtaking it. Henry swore with frustration.

"It's maddening," said Emmy soothingly, "but never mind. We've got plenty of time."

"That's just what we haven't got." Henry tooted his horn, not in the hope of achieving anything useful, but to relieve his feelings. "It's nearly a quarter to five, and I want to catch Samuel before he goes home. Also, I don't want to have to break into Sugar Mill House."

Henry managed to edge the Jeep past the truck at last, on the same stretch of road where the black car had passed him the day before, but by then it was five o'clock and still a good ten minutes' drive to Lucy's front door.

The Jeep swung at dangerous speed through the big gates and screeched to a halt on the gravel of the driveway. Henry jumped out and ran to the front door. It was locked, the shutters were closed, and the whole house had a deserted air.

"Dammit," he said, as Emmy joined him. "Now we'll have to try to find a window open or—"

He stopped abruptly. The front door was swinging silently open. And around it came Samuel's smiling black face.

"Samuel!" Emmy's relief was evident. "May we come in?"

"Come in and welcome, Miz Tibbett. But Miz Lucy not here."

"What are you doing here yourself, Samuel?" Henry asked. "It's well after five."

Samuel grinned. "When Miz Lucy not home, I sleep here. Take care, like. Some bad people 'roun here, break windows an' thieve when house empty." A little pause. "You want come in?"

Henry said, "If we may, Samuel. We're very puzzled that Miss Lucy should have gone off-island so suddenly. You had no idea of her plans?"

Samuel opened the door wide and stepped back to let Henry and Emmy into the sitting room. Instead of answering, he gestured toward the table, where a piece of paper lay weighted down by a sphere of white brain coral. Henry looked at it. Lucy's writing was unmistakable.

Samuel. My plans have changed suddenly and I am going off-island this evening. Not sure when I will be back. Please sleep in the house as usual until I return. Please telephone Mr. Bishop at Pirate's Cave and tell him I will be away for a few days.

L.P.D.

"Nothing else?" Henry was frowning as he looked at the note. Samuel shook his head. "I believe Miss Lucy had another visitor after we left. Do you know who it was?"

"No, sir. I was home at my supper."

There was no question of being able to search the house. Henry and Emmy were supposed to be no more than casual acquaintances of Lucy's, and although Samuel seemed completely trustworthy, he might easily be innocently indiscreet.

Henry decided to try another tactic. "Ah, well, that seems to be that. It's a pity, because I wanted to ask Miss Lucy about this new ferryboat. I suppose she traveled on it?"

Samuel's round face was entirely ingenuous. "I don't know sir. Like I said, I was home."

"When will the next boat be?" Henry asked.

"She come back down from Seawards tomorrow morning, stop here an' Tampica Harbour, then go on other islands." Samuel obviously enjoyed airing his local knowledge.

"I see. Well, could you show us where the jetty is?"

"Surely, sir." Samuel led them to the front door and out into the drive. Pointing through the open gate, he said, "Jus' follow the new road down to the sea. You'll see the wharf."

The wharf was not an elaborate affair. A simple wooden pier strode out into the water, terminating in a T-shaped section, which was clearly where the ferry moored. At the head of the pier was a small hut, now padlocked, which presumably served as a ticket office. The only human beings to be seen were a couple of small boys in ragged jeans, who were fishing with homemade rods and lines from the end of the jetty. In the deepening twilight, Henry and Emmy walked down to them.

The boys, who looked about six and eight years old, glanced up without much interest, then concentrated on their lines once more. Emmy said, "Caught anything?"

The elder of the boys shook his head shyly, then said, "You go boat?"

"Is there a boat?" Emmy asked.

The boy shook his head again. "Only my father boat. He go fish."

"Would your father take us in his boat?"

The boy looked up at Emmy, clearly not understanding the question. At that moment, the smaller boy jumped up, shouting excitedly.

76

"He reach! He reach!"

Instantly, both boys were on their feet, dancing with anticipation, and around the headland came a small whaler, powered by an outboard motor, throwing up a plume of white spray as it roared toward the jetty, then throttling back to, as the rangy black fisherman came alongside.

As Henry and Emmy watched, the boys gave their father a great welcome and helped him unload his catch—a few red snapper, some rainbow-gleaming parrot fish, and a netful of assorted smaller fry, which the West Indians call pot fish.

When the catch was ashore and the boat secured, the fisherman jumped lightly onto the jetty, and Henry approached him.

"Good evening. I see you've been out fishing."

The man smiled, attractively. "You want buy fish?"

"No thank you. Not today. I was really interested in the ferryboat to the Seawards."

"No boat this evenin'. Monday, Wednesday, Friday."

"I know," said Henry. "I'm trying to find out if a friend of ours took the ferry to the Seawards yesterday evening."

The man looked blank. "Friend o' yours?"

"Miss Lucy," said Henry.

The fisherman smiled again. "Ah, so you be frens Miz Lucy?"

"We don't know her very well—" Emmy began, hastily.

The fisherman scratched his head. "You say Miz Lucy go boat yesterday?"

"That's what we've been told."

"No, sir," The fisherman was very definite. "I'm here las' evenin'—reach late. I see boat go out. No Miz Lucy."

"You're absolutely sure?"

"No Miz Lucy." With an emphatic nod, the fisherman swung his bulging sack—which had once contained onions—

77

over his shoulder and strode away up the jetty, accompanied by his sons.

Henry and Emmy looked at each other in silence for a moment. Then Henry said, "It's pretty obvious, isn't it? Lucy was driven off somewhere by her mysterious visitor in the black government limousine."

"Do you think she wrote that note voluntarily, Henry?"

Henry grinned, a little ruefully. "It would be very difficult to force Lucy to write anything she didn't want to. Unless, of course—"

"Unless she did it to protect somebody else. Do you think she's really off-island?"

"She may be anywhere, blast her," said Henry. "Well, there's nothing more to be done here. We'd better get back before it gets completely dark. We can at least make a few inquiries at the airport and ferry dock. Somebody may have noticed her leaving."

"And in the meantime," said Emmy, "what about us?"

"What do you mean—what about us?"

"De Marco's threat. Do we stay on at Pirate's Cave?"

"We've got until tomorrow to think about that. We must talk to Ironmonger, for sure. And we must find Lucy."

It was a frustrating evening. By the time the Tibbetts got to the airport, the last plane had taken off, and the Terminal Building was dark and padlocked. They had no more luck at the ferry wharf. A call to Melinda's Market produced, unsurprisingly, no reply. Depressed, they went back to Pirate's Cave for dinner.

"Let's hope," said Henry, "that something happens in the morning."

7

The next morning dawned fresh and briskly breezy, with no hint of anything remotely sinister in the air. As they walked to the beach for a prebreakfast swim, it seemed to Henry and Emmy that De Marco's threat was no more than a joke, that Lucy Pontefract-Deacon was indeed away on a short visit to friends, and that Sir Edward's dark suspicions of the members of his government were simply figments of his imagination. The gardens of Pirate's Cave smelled green and sweet as sprinklers refreshed the lawns in the cool of the morning, and gardeners went about their tasks of raking gravel paths and snipping off yesterday's dead hibiscus heads.

At the beach, one or two early swimmers splashed in the crystal water, the sand was being raked and sunbeds arranged under the bohias, and Dolphin and his crew had the huge parachute laid out on a grassy bank and were inspecting it carefully prior to the day's sport. Impossible to imagine any force of evil in this idyllic place.

After their swim, the Tibbetts went back to their cottage, showered, and dressed for breakfast. Going into the dining room they met Tom Brinkman, who was coming out. He greeted them with a cordial wave.

"Good morning," said Emmy. "Off parasailing again?"

Brinkman grinned. "You bet. Can't waste a morning like this."

"Isn't there too much wind?" Henry asked.

"Nope. Just right. Be seein' ya."

Sure enough, before breakfast was over the Tibbetts saw that a small motor dinghy was taking Brinkman out to the raft, where the larger control boat was waiting. They watched as the harness was adjusted and the parachute made ready. Then Dolphin started the towboat, moving gently away from the raft, as the men on each side of Brinkman raised the parachute to take the wind. A moment later, the multicolored nylon filled, Dolphin revved up the boat, and Brinkman rose like a graceful bird into the clear air.

"It looks so beautiful," said Emmy. "I wish I had the guts to—"

She broke off abruptly. Something was wrong. Dolphin seemed to be fighting with the wheel of the towboat, which was now roaring ahead at high speed. But instead of respond-ing, the boat turned in a tight circle, much too fast, leaning over perilously.

Henry jumped to his feet. "Why doesn't he stop her?"

It was too late. The boat capsized in a fountain of spray, and Brinkman, under his collapsed parachute, plummeted three hundred feet into the water, like Icarus punished by the gods.

At once the beach became a scene of confusion. There were shouts, boats were launched, people seemed to appear from nowhere, all concentrated on the splash of color that was the parachute lying like an oil slick on the water.

By the time Henry and Emmy reached the beach, three men in a Boston whaler were already dragging Brinkman from the water, and a doctor—one of the hotel guests—was waiting onshore. But the big American was dead.

As the doctor straightened up from examining the body, Henry said to him, "What killed him, do you know?"

The doctor gave him a bleak and unfriendly look. "Too soon to be sure without an autopsy, but I'd say he broke his neck when he hit the water. He certainly didn't drown." He turned to the circle of hotel employees who were staring, appalled and incredulous. "Okay you men, get him onto one of these sunbeds and carry him up to the hotel. Call the hospital for an ambulance. Get moving, everybody."

The capsized towboat was floating aimlessly around the bay, drifting ever closer to the reef on the receding tide. Henry saw that Dolphin had been brought ashore and was sitting on the beach, his dark curly head in his hands and his shoulders heaving with great sobs. It was, Henry knew, the worst calamity that could have happened to him. And not just a personal disaster. The reputation of Pirate's Cave, in fact the whole image of tourism on Tampica would be bound to suffer. For a moment, Henry hoped that it might be more than a tragic accident. If it could be proved that the boat had been tampered with . . .

He shouted to the men in the whaler. "For God's sake, go and get that towboat before it breaks up on the reef!"

The men seemed to come out of a trance and were suddenly galvanized into action. It was very nearly too late. The towboat, swept by the strong wind, had already crashed onto the coral, and there was a cracking sound as she was pounded again and again on the sharp spikes just below the surface. Eventually, however, the crew of the whaler managed to get a rope around her rudder and, with difficulty, dragged the battered craft to shore.

They were hauling it up onto the beach when Patrick Bishop appeared from among the trees, accompanied by

Police Commissioner Kelly. Bishop came straight over to Henry.

"Did you see exactly what happened, Mr. Tibbett?"

"I saw what happened," said Henry, "but I don't know why it happened. Perhaps Dolphin can tell us."

Bishop went over to the boatman, who was still sitting motionless, his head in his hands. Gently, he put a hand on the man's shoulder and said, "Tell us, Dolphin. What happened?"

Dolphin shook his head, without uncovering his face.

Again Bishop said, "You must tell me, Dolphin."

This time Dolphin raised his head very slowly, and Henry saw the expression of sheer primitive terror on his face. He whispered something to Bishop and then, without warning, took to his heels and ran off among the trees, as if pursued by demons.

Briskly, Commissioner Kelly said, "What did he say, Patrick?"

The manager sighed. "What do you think? He says the bad obeah-man put a spell on the boat. You can see he's scared out of his wits. He thinks he's doomed to die, and he very well may be."

"Do people really still believe that superstitious nonsense?" Emmy asked.

Bishop and Kelly exchanged an uneasy glance but said nothing. The awkward silence was broken by Henry, who was squatting beside the damaged boat.

"Come and look at this." He stood up. "This was nothing to do with obeah-men. Somebody deliberately wrecked the steering."

"How?" demanded Kelly.

"The rudder is controlled by a wire, which passes over a pulley and up to the wheel. It's broken."

82

Angrily, Bishop said, "That's not possible."

"Look for yourself," said Henry. "It's broken and the ends are frayed."

Bishop lifted up the broken wire and shook his head in disbelief. "Dolphin checks the boat from stem to stern every morning before he takes it out. He couldn't possibly have missed this."

"My guess," said Henry, "is that the wire was filed so that it was still holding, but only by a few strands. Then the frayed place was probably covered by a small piece of silver tape. I don't suppose you'll ever find—yes, by God, I believe that's it." He leaned into the boat and picked something up off the cockpit floor. "What a bit of luck. Well, there you have it. The steering would have appeared in perfect order on a trial run, and it would have taken a virtual overhaul of the boat to spot the damage. I really don't think you can blame Dolphin."

Kelly turned to Bishop. "You see what this means, Patrick?"

Bishop gave a rueful grin. "I'm trying not to," he said. "I suppose you mean a full police investigation."

"I'm afraid so. Now, could anybody have known that Brinkman would be the first person to go parasailing this morning?"

"That's easy," said Henry. "He was almost the only hotel guest who did it, and he was always out first in the morning."

"So it looks like a deliberate attack on Mr. Brinkman."

"He might easily not have been killed, Desmond," Bishop pointed out. "That was very bad luck. These accidents have happened before, and—"

"Perhaps," said Henry, "this was a demonstration to frighten him. Or perhaps," he added, to Bishop, "it was to sabotage your hotel. In any case, I presume it'll be treated as a criminal matter."

83

Kelly said, "It is a very unfortunate occurrence, Mr. Tibbett, but please do not let it disturb your holiday. After all, police matters are not exactly in your sphere, are they?" He smiled. "Well, Patrick, let's go up to your office. We'll have to try and find out who did this. Thank you for your help, Mr. Tibbett . . . good day . . ."

The two men bowed politely and made their way back to the hotel.

"Let's get back to the cottage," Henry said to Emmy.

When they were inside and decently soundproofed, Emmy said, "Well? What now?"

"We'll have to split up."

"How do you mean?"

"I don't pretend to understand what's going on," Henry said, "but I'm extremely worried about Lucy."

"Just what I was thinking."

"Lucy can be your assignment. I want you to get away from here and find her."

"And what will you do?"

"I shall stay here and try to get to the bottom of this murder, if I can."

"Henry, remember what De Marco—"

"That's all changed now. If Brinkman was De Marco's man, as he obviously must have been—"

"He'll think that you killed Brinkman," said Emmy grimly. "That'll put you on top of his list for extermination."

"All part of the job, darling." Henry grinned at her, and she stuck her tongue out at him. Henry sometimes played a little game of mock heroics, which did not amuse her. "Actually, I think the safest place I can be at the moment is right here. I think even De Marco might think that two fatal accidents at the same hotel within a few days would call for comment. Meanwhile, I must talk to Dolphin. And to Sir Edward."

"And me? Where do I start?"

Henry considered. "The airport, I think. They may not keep very efficient passenger manifestos, but Lucy is a well-known figure. I think anybody who was on duty on Monday evening would remember if she had taken a flight out. If you draw a blank there, check Sugar Mill House again, and if she's not back, you'd better go to the Seawards yourself. You know Lucy's friends there."

"Why can't I just telephone?"

"Because—"

"Because," said Emmy, "you know very well that it's dangerous here, and you're determined to get rid of me."

"All right, perhaps I am. But I'm also determined to find Lucy. So we'll take the Jeep and drive to Tampica Harbour. You can drop me at a call box, and I'll phone Sir Edward, while you go on to the airport and, if necessary, to Sugar Mill House and anywhere else you need to go. Don't worry about me."

"Don't worry?" said Emmy gloomily. "You're an optimist. For heaven's sake, take care."

Emmy deposited Henry at the row of telephones outside the post office and drove out of the town along the road to the airport. If only, she thought, it had still been the tiny airstrip and little concrete building of their first visit, everything would have been easy. Now, with jets arriving from the States and Europe, and a proliferation of personnel and airline desks, she felt that there was little hope that anybody would remember an individual traveler.

Then she cheered up a little. If Lucy had left Tampica

85

voluntarily, it was unlikely that she had gone far. Most likely to a nearby island, most probably the Seawards. Emmy resolved that she would start her search among the small local airlines.

The girl at the British Seaward Airways desk was beautiful, black, and slender as a reed. She wore a nametag reading ILICIA MURPHY. At the moment she was applying a coat of silver varnish to her inch-long fingernails. She barely looked up at Emmy's query.

"Miss Lucy Pontefract-Deacon," Emmy said again. "You must know her. Everybody does."

Ilicia studied her nails with rapt attention. She said, "I'm from the Seawards. I don't know people here."

"Well, were you on duty on Monday evening?"

The girl raised her hand and turned it this way and that, the better to admire the tapering black fingers with their brilliant metallic tips. She said, simply, "No."

"Do you know who was?"

A sigh. "No."

"Well, would there be any records of—"

At that moment, an American family arrived—a young couple with two small children, waving passports and tickets. Ilicia gave Emmy a perfunctory smile, said, "Excuse me," and moved off down the counter to attend to these bona fide travelers.

Emmy then tried Inter-Island Air, Blue Caribbean Charters, and Sunshine Airways. Inter-Island had no flights after five-thirty on Monday evenings. Blue Caribbean had had no charters that day. Sunshine Airways had had a commuter flight to several islands at 6:15, and the girl knew Lucy by sight. She was positive that the old lady had not been on the plane. It seemed that if Lucy had left Tampica for another

Caribbean island on Monday evening, it could only have been on the British Seaward flight at 7:15, but there seemed to be no way of proving it.

The large intercontinental airlines stored passenger lists in their computers, but their desks were busy and they had no intention of furnishing information. In any case, it was highly unlikely that Lucy would have flown off to London, Miami, or New York.

Emmy sighed and went back to the Jeep. There seemed nothing to do but to follow Henry's next instruction and drive over to Sugar Mill House. As she left the airport, she noticed that the girl at British Seaward Airways had picked up her phone and had begun to dial, but she thought nothing of it.

Melinda's Market answered Henry's call promptly. The same soft-spoken lady very much regretted that it would be impossible for Mr. Scott to speak to Edward. Edward, she explained, was off-island.

This, felt Henry, was the last straw. "When will he be back, do you know?"

"I'm sorry, Mr. Scott. He didn't say."

"Do you know where he's gone?"

There was a hesitation. "I don't know surely, but likely British Seawards."

"Oh, well. I'll try him again tomorrow."

"You do that, Mr. Scott. You do that."

Deeply discouraged, Henry hung up. The absence of both Sir Edward and Lucy was not only sinister; it left him feeling ineffective and defenseless. All he could do now was go back to the hotel and try a different line of investigation.

Henry found Patrick Bishop's secretary glued to the telephone in the outer office. She waved him to a seat, put her hand over the telephone speaker, and said briefly, "Long distance. Sorry." Then, into the telephone. "Is that Miami, Florida, Directory Assistance? . . . Good . . . Yes, I would like the telephone number of Mr. Thomas Brinkman . . . B as in Baker . . . That's right . . . 3261 Shoreline Drive . . . Yes, I'll hold . . . What's that? But there must be . . . Well, maybe he didn't have a telephone, but . . . Now, that's ridiculous! I mean . . . No, I wasn't trying to be rude . . . Yes, I suppose you should know . . . Well, thanks anyway."

She hung up and turned in exasperation to Henry, the nearest human being. "What do you know?" she demanded. "The girl in Miami says there's no such address!"

"People have been known to give false addresses to hotels," Henry remarked.

"Well, I shall have to tell Mr. Bishop. I don't know what we do now."

"Wait for *Bellissima* to come back," Henry suggested. "Mr. De Marco's boat. He was Mr. Brinkman's friend."

"It's all very unsatisfactory."

"It must be." Henry was sympathetic. "Just before you go and tell Mr. Bishop, could you give me an address?"

"An address?"

"I'm trying to find Dolphin, the boatman," Henry explained. "I think he's probably at home."

"Dolphin Carruthers? He doesn't have an exact address. Lives with his mother along the road to Tampica Harbour. Second white house on the left after you leave the Pirate's Cave grounds."

Henry said, "Thank you very much." Then, "Carruthers, did you say? Any relation to the Prime Minister?"

The secretary flashed a smile. "Carruthers is a big, big title here, Mr. Tibbett. Like Kelly and Murphy. Back in slave days, slaves took their master's title. That's why the *name* is important."

Henry remembered that in the West Indies, the surname is the title, and the given name, the name. The secretary's explanation also helped him to understand the often fanciful names West Indian parents give their children. With comparatively few titles on the island, it was essential that names should be distinctive. He thanked the secretary again, but she barely heard him. She was already going into the manager's office to explain to Mr. Bishop that Brinkman had given a fictitious address in the hotel register, and that it would not be possible to contact next of kin.

Henry found the white house with no difficulty. It was an old-fashioned West Indian dwelling made of slatted wood, with a steeply pitched galvanized roof painted red, and royal blue shutters. The yard around it was as neat as a pin and inhabited by several hens, scraping busily for tidbits in the dust, and a few goats who stood up elegantly on their back legs to reach tasty morsels from the tops of shrubs, as goats and rams have done ever since 3000 B.C., as Sir Leonard Woolley demonstrated by his findings at Ur. There seemed to be nobody about. Henry unlatched the gate of the compound and went in. The shutters were open and the breeze ruffled the bright chintz curtains, which made it impossible to see inside; but there was no sound.

Henry called, "Anybody home?"

Silence.

"Mistress Carruthers?" Henry remembered just in time the correct West Indian form of address to a married lady.

Very slowly the door began to open, and around it crept a wizened black arm. This was followed by a tiny old lady. Her back was bent and her thin legs obviously found even hobbling difficult. She wore a shapeless blue dress, and her traditional head scarf did not succeed in covering all of her springy gray hair. She said, "Who be you?"

"I'm looking for Dolphin."

"Dolphin in enough trouble, he. You go now."

"Mistress Carruthers—"

"*Miss* Marciette, if you please. I ain't never been married." The old lady sniffed, and added with pride, "No more was my mother."

"I'm so sorry, Miss Marciette. I didn't mean to insult you. But you are Dolphin's mother, right?"

"Doan talk me 'bout Dolphin."

"He's here, in the house?"

"He dere til he die, and dat's de troot."

"He's not going to die, Miss Marciette."

The old lady turned her head away. "I promise you," Henry added.

Still with averted face, Miss Marciette said, "What you know 'bout it? You doan know nuttin'."

"I was there when the accident happened this morning. It wasn't Dolphin's fault, Miss Marciette."

"Sure, warn't his fault." Miss Marciette spat on the ground. "But he goin' go die of it, like the 'Merican gentleman."

Henry said, "Please, Miss Marciette, let me see your son."

There was a long pause. Then the woman said, "I goin' feed de pigs and dem. You go in if you want. He won't speak. You see."

Very slowly she shuffled across the yard, picked up a bucket, and disappeared around the back of the house. Tentatively, Henry pushed aside the cretonne curtain and went inside.

It was very dark in the little house after the brilliance of the sunshine outside. Henry was surprised at the tininess of the room into which he stepped—little wider than a corridor, with just enough space for a cooking stove and a sink—both of which, he noticed were shiny and new. A curtained doorway led into another, slightly larger room, furnished with a plastic-topped table and matching chairs, an elaborately carved cupboard, and a large television set. Off it to the left led yet another curtained doorway, and it was beyond this that Henry found himself in a miniscule bedroom. Virtually the only piece of furniture was the bed, and on it lay a figure hunched into the fetal position, face to the wall, and covered by a floral-patterned sheet.

"Dolphin," said Henry softly.

The figure on the bed did not move or react in any way.

"Dolphin, it's Mr. Tibbett. Please talk to me." Silence. "Dolphin, what you think isn't true. Mr. Brinkman's death had nothing to do with an obeah-man."

At that, Dolphin pulled the sheet even more tightly around him, and let out a little moan. Henry sat down on the bed. "Listen to me, Dolphin. It wasn't your fault. And it wasn't obeah. Somebody deliberately cut the steering wire on your boat." Another low moan. "For heaven's sake, man, an obeah-man wouldn't need to cut a wire with a knife. He'd work by magic—isn't that right? Your enemy isn't any sort of a magician—he's an ordinary, wicked human being."

For a moment Henry thought he was not going to get any response. Then, however, Dolphin stirred, and one eye, rolling in fear, peeped around the edge of the sheet.

"Best you keep 'way, Mr. Tibbett. Is danger."

"There well may be danger, if you don't pull yourself together," said Henry briskly. "There's a murderer about, and you can help catch him, instead of lying there imagining that you're under some sort of a spell."

From under the sheets, Henry could just make out some words "What you say . . . not possible . . . every morning . . . boat check . . ."

"I know you check the boat every morning, Dolphin. And I'm sure you did so this morning, and everything was fine. But the murderer didn't cut all the way through the wire, and you wouldn't have noticed anything wrong on a trial run. It was only with the pressure of the parachute that the last strands parted, and the steering went. Your boat wasn't bewitched. It was sabotaged."

Again the eye peeped out. "Is de troot?"

"The truth, Dolphin. Now, come out from under, make up your mind that you're not going to die, and tell me what happened."

Knowing a little of the deep and secret streams of magic lore that run just below the surface in all West Indians, Henry had doubts whether he would succeed, but Dolphin was a very intelligent young man and he trusted Henry. Little by little, he raised his head, pushed back the sheet, and at last was sitting up beside Henry, talking.

What emerged was little more than Henry already knew. The boat had been inspected and tested, as usual, and everything had appeared to be in order. Mr. Brinkman had more or less monopolized the parasailing crew over the past week or so, and was inevitably the first out every morning. It was patently obvious that he had been the intended victim.

As to the accident itself, Henry was fascinated to hear Dolphin's explanation. He had not realized that, with the parachute acting as a sort of remote sail, the towboat had to behave as a sailboat rather than a motorboat, tacking against the wind, reaching with the wind on the beam, and running before it. As with a sailboat, the last was by far the trickiest point for the helmsman, as he had to be on the lookout for an accidental jibe—that is, for the wind to cross his stern unexpectedly. With the steering gear out of operation, this is what had happened. The jibe had caused the parachute to collapse and plummet into the sea. The drag of the water-logged parachute had capsized the out-of-control towboat. The unfortunate parasailor had gone into the water underneath the parachute and became completely entangled in its ropes, still being dragged along by the crazed motorboat. People had survived such mishaps, but not very often. If the accident had not actually killed Brinkman, it would at least have given him a very severe fright—the sort of grim warning that was evidently intended.

Henry said, "Have you any idea at all of who could have done this, Dolphin?"

Dolphin shrugged. "Plenty bad people. Plenty doan like me."

"You must get it out of your head," said Henry patiently, "that this was directed against you. It was Mr. Brinkman who died, wasn't it?"

"Obeah-man doan go after 'Mericans."

"Look, we've been into all that. There was no obeah-man."

Dolphin said nothing, but looked sideways at Henry. At last he spoke. "I see he."

"You saw him? Who was it?"

"Doan know."

"Tell me exactly what you saw, and when."

After another long pause, Dolphin said, "Early mornin'. Not proper day yet. I comin' down early for check boat. I see man runnin' away into trees."

"You're certain? You saw a man running away from the beach, near the boat, and disappearing into the trees?" Dolphin nodded. "Did you recognize him?" Dolphin shook his head. "Well, can you describe him?"

"A small man."

Henry knew that when a West Indian uses the word "small," he means thin rather than short. "How tall was he?" Dolphin made a rocking gesture with his hand to indicate average height. "Did you see what he was wearing?"

"Trousers. Like blue jean. T-shirt, dark color." Suddenly Dolphin began to tremble. In a whisper, he added, "Blood."

"What do you mean, blood?"

Dolphin was now shivering uncontrollably. "He hand . . . he foot . . . blood . . . I see . . . So I know he be obeah-man. . . ."

Henry put his arm around the young man's shoulder.

"Dolphin," he said, "please listen to me. There wasn't any blood. The sun was just coming up, and it throws strange shadows and makes strange colors. That was no obeah-man. That was a criminal, and his weapons were not magic, but hatred in his heart and a knife in his hand." He paused. "Was he a black man?"

Dolphin nodded. "No white obeah-man."

"And thank God for it," Henry said. He added, "We had them once, you know."

Dolphin looked up, suddenly interested. Henry went on. "But we found a better magic, and we drove them out."

"Is troot?"

"Truth, Dolphin. And what we found wasn't really magic. You know all about it. Science. Not so long ago, people would have thought that your boat ran by magic."

Dolphin laughed.

"And," Henry went on, "what about radio and television? And aeroplanes? And spacecraft?"

"Strong magic, Mr. Tibbett. You right. We have strong magic."

"Of course you do. So just forget about the other kind, will you? And no more talk of dying. Okay?"

He held out his hand and Dolphin grasped it, just as Miss Marciette came hobbling around the corner of the house, carrying her empty bucket. She took one look at Henry and Dolphin through the open window, dropped the bucket, and held her hands up to heaven. Then she hurried into the house on uncertain feet and seized one of Henry's hands in both of hers.

"Great obeah-man! Great powerful obeah-man! T'ank you. T'ank you. You take bad spell off my son!"

It seemed too complicated to explain. Henry just smiled at her and left.

8

Emmy was feeling discouraged. One look at Sugar Mill House, as she drove into the driveway, was enough to tell her that the place was deserted. The shutters were fastened and the front door closed.

The sound of the car, however, must have alerted Samuel, for he appeared from the back of the house and greeted Emmy with his usual broad grin.

"Miz Lucy still away, Miz Tibbett."

"You've had no word from her?"

Samuel shook his head. "She stay maybe three, four day."

Emmy sighed. Henry's next instruction was to go and look for Lucy in the Seaward Islands, and this she was extremely reluctant to do. She was more than half convinced that it would be a wild-goose chase, simply designed to get her away from Tampica to the safety of friends, while Henry stayed to face the music. Still, orders were orders, and she was about to restart the Jeep when Samuel suddenly raised his head.

"Listen!"

"Listen to what?"

"The boat reach."

By then Emmy, too, could hear the steady throb of engines approaching the jetty. "From the Seawards?" she asked.

"Sure."

"Then maybe she's on it!" Emmy revved up the Jeep and headed for the landing stage.

By the time she got there, the ferry was maneuvering alongside with much chattering and laughter, as nimble boys jumped ashore with ropes. Then the gangplank came down with a clatter, a crew member opened the ship's door, and passengers began to disembark.

Lucy was one of the first ashore. She sailed gracefully down the gangway, her cotton skirt billowing, followed by a diminutive boy in a huge cap, who was carrying her suitcase. After him came a few smartly dressed local people, back from visiting friends and relatives on other islands, and a handful of pale-skinned tourists bound for the new local hotels; but it was clear that Sugar Mill Bay was only a whistle-stop. The great majority of the passengers were going to Tampica Harbour.

Emmy jumped out of the Jeep and ran to greet the old lady. "Oh, Lucy, I'm so glad to see you!"

"My dear child, what on earth are you doing here?" Lucy sounded surprised and not overpleased.

"I've so much to tell you, Lucy. Get in the Jeep and I'll drive you home."

"Oh, very well. Yes, Herbert, you may put my case into that Jeep. Thank you very much, dear. Go and buy yourself an ice cream." A coin changed hands, and the boy scampered off. With some ceremony, Lucy climbed into the passenger seat, and the two women drove the short distance to Sugar Mill House.

Once inside, Lucy began touring the house, throwing wide the shutters and switching on the big-bladed wooden fans. Feeling somewhat silly and very much one down, Emmy trotted after her.

"We've been so worried, Lucy. We had no idea you were going away—"

Lucy flung wide another shutter. "Didn't Samuel tell Patrick Bishop, as I asked him to?"

"Yes, yes, he did. But—"

"Well, then. There was surely nothing very unusual in my paying a short visit to the British Seawards. You know I have many friends there."

"I know, but—"

"You remember Dr. Duncan, who used to work here?"

"Of course I do."

"Well, he has retired at last and gone to the Seawards. I was visiting him, among other people."

"I never thought he'd leave Tampica," said Emmy. She was remembering the Irish doctor who had worked all his life to bring modern medical care to Tampica, and in whose honor the fine new hospital was named.

Lucy hooked open the last shutter. "Nor did I," she said dryly, "and nor did he. But he didn't like what he saw happening to this island, and the new government didn't like him. So Eddie and I stayed, and Alfred helps us from a discreet distance." She turned to face Emmy. "So—why are you here?"

"I hardly know where to start." Emmy pushed back a strand of black hair from her forehead. She suddenly felt very tired. "Thomas Brinkman is dead."

"No great loss," said Lucy tartly. "What happened?"

Emmy told her.

"An accident?"

"Henry doesn't think so, but some people want it to seem so."

"Who, for example?"

"The hotel, for one."

Lucy's eyebrows went up. "The hotel? I would doubt

that. Murder isn't the management's fault. An accident is."

"Well, Mr. Bishop didn't seem at all keen on an investigation. Nor, I think, did Commissioner Kelly—but Henry was able to show that the boat had been sabotaged—so obviously there'll have to be an inquiry. But you haven't heard the half of it yet."

"Then let us sit down, and Samuel will bring us a drink." Lucy seemed more relaxed. She rang a small silver bell, which produced Samuel from the kitchen. "Rum punch, Emmy dear? Two rum punches, please, Samuel. Everything been all right while I was away?"

"Yes, Miz Lucy. Sure, Miz Lucy."

Relaxing over her drink, Emmy explained about the *Bellissima*, the supposed rendezvous, Sir Edward's luncheon, the tape recorder, and finally the debacle and De Marco's threats.

Lucy listened in silence. Then she said, "I told you I didn't trust that man! Yachting caps and blazers!"

Emmy said, "Henry won't budge from Pirate's Cave. *Bellissima* will be back either today or tomorrow. When De Marco hears that Brinkman is dead—"

"He will doubtless be annoyed," said Lucy. "What about Eddie? What does he say?"

"I don't know. Henry was going to contact him by phone this morning, while I tried to trace you."

The old lady smiled. "And did you succeed? In tracing me, I mean."

"No," said Emmy, "but I can make a good guess. You were driven to the airport on Monday evening by whoever visited you after we left—the person in the black government limousine, who we know wasn't Sir Edward. You must have taken the seven-fifteen British Seaward flight. The girl at the desk—Ilicia Murphy—told me that she wasn't on duty on

Monday evening, and that anyway she's from the Seawards and wouldn't have recognized you, but I don't think she was telling the truth. Why, I can't imagine. Anyhow, there was no other flight you could have taken, and we know you didn't take the boat."

Lucy smiled and nodded. "You are as good a detective as Henry," she said. "Now I suppose you want me to explain."

"Not if it was something private." Emmy was embarrassed. "I mean, if it had nothing to do with the drug situation—"

"I'm afraid it had." Lucy sounded very sad. "I would have preferred to keep it to myself, but I am sure I can trust in your discretion. You may tell Henry, but nobody else. You understand?"

"Of course."

"Well, then." Lucy stirred her drink with a slender glass stick. "My visitor was Carmelita Carruthers. The Prime Minister's wife. You have met her?"

"Yes. Twice. The second time, at the Palmers' house, I thought she looked ill. Ill and unhappy."

"You were quite right, Emmy. She came to me on Monday as a last resort, I suppose. You know how people do."

"I know, Lucy."

"You can guess why?"

Emmy remembered. "Drugs," she said. "I noticed at the Palmers' that she seemed to have a bad cold. That's a sign, isn't it?"

"Cocaine," said Lucy. "Known locally as the white girl. An unfortunate euphemism."

"Has she been on it for long?"

"I fear so."

"But why was she in such a state? I mean, it must be easy to get here."

"That," said Lucy, "is what is so interesting. Carmelita confirmed that Brinkman was in the process of arranging a big drug deal with her husband and others. Just the evidence we need, but, of course, quite useless coming from her. She also told me that it's not the first time such a thing has happened. Chester doesn't know about Carmelita's habit. He has the sense to stay off the stuff himself—he just makes money out of wretched addicts. But Carmelita was always able to get whatever she wanted from Chester's American contacts. Until now."

Emmy's eyes opened wide. "And Brinkman wouldn't play?"

"That's Carmelita's story. Of course, she knows who the local pushers are—but she dare not go to them. Chester would almost certainly find out, and she's very much afraid of him. She was close to suicide when she came to me."

Emmy said, "So you didn't go to the Seawards to see Dr. Duncan at all."

"Oh, yes, I did. The only fib I told you was when I said that Alfred had retired. It should have been semiretired. He still has an active interest in a new venture on St. Mark's—a rehabilitation clinic for addicts. I persuaded Carmelita to let me take her there."

"Does her husband know where she is?"

Lucy grinned. "I called him from the Seawards and told him that Carmelita was visiting with friends of mine, and might be away for quite a while."

"What was his reaction?"

"As a matter of fact," said Lucy, "he didn't seem very interested. My guess is that he has more serious things to worry about."

"She surely should stay at the clinic for a long time," Emmy said.

Lucy sipped her drink. "What she should do and what she will do are very different things. She'll stay until she feels better—which probably means, until she can get her hands on some cocaine. At which point she'll come home. It's very depressing, but it happens all too often." There was a little pause, and then Lucy said, "So Henry thinks that Brinkman was murdered."

Emmy hesitated. "Someone certainly set up a bad accident for him. Whoever did it couldn't be sure that he'd be killed, but there was a very good chance of it. Either way, it was obviously intended to get him off this island."

"I shall have to speak to Eddie about this." Lucy sounded worried. "When did you say *Bellissima* was expected back?"

"Today or tomorrow."

"It's very annoying. I shall have to risk calling Eddie through Melinda, which I don't like doing. Excuse me a moment, my dear. My telephone is in my bedroom."

Lucy was back in a couple of minutes. She looked very grim. "As Henry will have discovered by now," she said, "Eddie is off-island, probably on the Seawards, for an indefinite stay. Or that's what Melinda has been told to say. I don't like this at all, Emmy. Not one little bit."

Emmy said, "I'd better get back to Pirate's Cave."

"You'd better stay right where you are, dear."

"What do you mean?"

"Exactly what I say. It would be extremely imprudent for you to go back to Pirate's Cave. Oh, confound Eddie! Yes, I mean it! What a time to go off-island!"

"So what do we do now?" Emmy asked.

Lucy began pacing the room. Fiercely, she said, "Nothing. That's what is so maddening. You must know by now, Emmy, that I am extremely bad at doing nothing."

—

As Henry made his way on foot from Dolphin's house back to the hotel, he saw *Bellissima.* He came over the crest of the hill that overlooked the bay just as the anchor chain was rattling through the hawser under the supervision of young Randy Porter. Henry stopped and watched. As soon as Randy was satisfied that the yacht was securely anchored, he let down the boarding ladder and hauled the rubber dinghy round from the stern. A minute later, he and De Marco were both on their way to the shore.

At the landing stage, Randy Porter put a painter round a bollard and steadied the whaler as De Marco climbed ashore. Then the young crewman settled back in the dinghy, lit a cigarette, and put his feet up on the thwart, obviously waiting to ferry his skipper back aboard.

Meanwhile, De Marco did not start up across the lawns to the hotel building, but instead turned and walked along the beach. He soon disappeared behind the screen of palm trees and shrubs.

Henry was intrigued. He waited for a couple of minutes, but when De Marco did not reappear, he made his way slowly down through the gardens to his cottage. Before he had the door more than a crack open, an American voice from inside said, "Good day, Mr. Tibbett."

Henry went in, leaving the door open behind him. De Marco was sitting in one of the rattan armchairs, looking very much at ease. He had a small gun in his hand.

"Please come in and shut the door behind you, Mr. Tibbett."

Without moving, Henry said, "What are you doing here?"

De Marco smiled. "The question is rather—what are *you* doing here, Mr. Tibbett? I thought my instructions were quite clear."

"They were."

"Then—I really must ask you to shut that door." De Marco made a little gesture with the gun. "Even though the next-door cottage is regrettably unoccupied, I have no intention of being overheard."

Henry shut the door.

"That's better. Now Mr. Tibbett, first things first. Did you kill Tom Brinkman?"

"Of course not."

"I don't think there is any 'of course' about it. You came here expressly to get rid of him. Who is paying you?"

With irritation, Henry said, "Nobody is paying me. I'm on holiday."

"I think we can drop that fiction, Tibbett. Where is your wife?"

"At this moment, I have no idea. I left her shopping in Tampica Harbour."

There was a little pause. Then De Marco said, "You have been making a great nuisance of yourself. I warned you to keep your nose out of this affair, and instead you got yourself deeper into it. If it transpires that you did kill Brinkman, your conduct is inexcusable. Inexcusable and, what is worse, unprofessional."

Henry said, "I've already told you, I had nothing to do with it. In fact, I—" he stopped.

"You were more interested in keeping him alive. Exactly." De Marco suddenly stood up, smiled broadly, transferred his gun to his left hand, and extended his right. "Forgive my little bit of play-acting just now, Chief Superintendent. I think we should introduce ourselves. I am Maurice Wright of the U.S. Drug Enforcement Agency. Pleased to know you." He reached into the pocket of his slacks. "My credentials."

"You expect me to believe you?"

"Here. Take a look." He showed an official identity card.

Henry studied it for a moment. Then he said, "These things can be forged."

"I very much doubt it. However, you are quite right to be cautious. Now try this on for size."

De Marco pulled an envelope from the breast pocket of his blazer. It was made of thick paper and sealed on the back with red sealing wax. The unbroken wax showed the seal of the Justice Department of the United States.

"Open it. I'm not likely to need it now."

Henry broke the seal. Inside was a highly official document, which, when stripped of its legalities, informed all those whom it might concern that Drug Enforcement Agent Maurice Wright, alias Maurizio De Marco, and Drug Enforcement Agent Ernest Stevenson, alias Thomas Brinkman, were empowered to effect arrests of suspected persons anywhere on United States territory—this territory being understood to include the motor yacht *Bellissima*, registered in the United States. It was signed by the United States Attorney General.

Henry said, "Where does young Randy Porter come into this?"

Wright shrugged. "He doesn't. He knows nothing about it. I needed a crew and the agency wasn't about to give me one. Randy is the son of an old friend of mine, and he's a fine seaman. Of course, before we actually make the bust, he would have to go. Meanwhile, what he doesn't know, he can't blab about. I shall send him home as soon as we get the boat back to the Seawards. I'm leaving her there for the time being."

There was a long pause. Then Henry handed back the

paper and the identity card, and said, "I seem to have made a bloody fool of myself. Why didn't you tell—?"

"Tell whom, Chief Superintendent? Is there anybody on Tampica who is to be trusted?"

"Sir Edward Ironmonger," said Henry.

"You think so? I am not at all so sure. However, I suggest that we sit down and think things over—now that we know we are on the same side, so to speak."

"I suggest," said Henry, "that we have a drink. I need it."

"Good idea." Wright dropped his gun on the table. "Got any Scotch?"

"Only rum, I'm afraid. With the makings of a punch."

"Make mine rum and orange then." As Henry went to the refrigerator, Wright crossed his long legs, and said, "You can appreciate now why you were such an infernal nuisance to us."

"I can indeed." Henry was busy with ice and glasses. "Of course, if I'd had the faintest idea—"

"Everything was going very smoothly. We've had our eye on this island for a long time. Our break came when we got information that, as we had suspected, the heads of the police and government were involved."

"Information?" Henry stopped, with the rum bottle upraised. "Where from? From the island?"

"Anonymous," said Wright tersely. "I guess from Tampica." He grinned. "The boys up top don't always tell me everything. I'm just the guy on the ground. I get my orders."

"Here." Henry handed the American a tall glass. "So, what exactly was your plan?"

"Cheers." Wright took a long drink, and set down the glass. "Well, we got lucky, because we were able to identify the last lot of Mafia boys who did a deal here. They were negotiating on behalf of the really big guy—a South American drug baron. We found out that he had decided to drop the Tampica connection and use another route—which left this place wide open for a fresh deal.

"Ernie and I picked the boat up in the Seawards, and I put him off in Tampica Harbour and cruised around, while he made the first approaches. He was able to set the ball rolling by dropping names—my pal Mario Bianco, or whatever, was here last year, right? Well, I'm in the same outfit, and I'm into the same sort of deal. You get it?"

Henry nodded. "And they fell for it?"

"They were very cautious at first. So many of these guys have gotten busted recently that we have to be a bit clever. You don't find them falling for the 'Just come over to Miami and we'll fix it there' line anymore. We had just about gotten them to agree to come aboard *Bellissima* when —"

"When I came and bitched everything up," said Henry.

"I was going to say, poor old Ernie died. Or was killed. Which was it, do you know?"

"A bit of both, I should say."

"What's that supposed to mean?"

"The boat was sabotaged. No doubt at all about that. It was done in such a way as to provoke the worst accident that can happen to a parasailor. But although an unintentional jibe will always bring the parachute down, you can't be sure that the man will be killed. Some people have been lucky."

"So you think it was more of a warning shot, do you?"

"Yes," said Henry, "I do."

"Well, whatever it was, I'm afraid we're exploded. Ernie and I and the *Bellissima*. Somebody's rumbled us."

"If I had anything to do with it . . ." Henry was deeply embarrassed.

Wright smiled. "I doubt it, buddy. I doubt it very much. However, if you have a guilty conscience and want to make amends, there's a very simple way of doing it."

"What's that?"

"Can I have another drink?"

"Of course." Henry was on his feet. "Same again?"

"Sure. Thanks. Now, listen. It won't have been missed that you and I are on bad terms. I also gather from my spies that you are posing as a very rich man, apparently willing to invest money in the island. You are ostensibly English, but the Tampicans know perfectly well that Englishmen as rich as that are as rare as hen's teeth. I'm talking about Mafia-rich. So the setup is all there. You are indeed English—a clever disguise—but you are working for a rival concern. You have an even better proposition to put to the Tampicans than we did." He paused, and took a swig at his fresh drink. "How does it appeal to you?"

"I can't say that it appeals to me at all." Henry was being honest. "On the other hand, I can see the advantages. And I feel I owe it to you. But surely there must be legal difficulties. I'm a British policeman. I've got no mandate to work for the United States Drug Enforcement Agency."

Wright stretched out his long legs and smiled. "You'd be surprised."

"What do you mean?"

"Your narcotics division and the DEA are cooperating very closely these days. I've just gotten back from the British Seawards. I saw the Governor while I was there. Thought I'd better take out an insurance policy on you, in case you refused to stop your unofficial activities."

"What sort of insurance policy?"

"Just this." Wright produced yet another envelope from his pocket. It was addressed to Henry Tibbett. "It's for you."

In the envelope was a letter, handwritten on the letterhead writing paper of Government House, St. Marks, British Seaward Islands. Henry recognized the handwriting and signature of the Governor.

Dear Chief Superintendent,

I have been in touch on the telephone with your Chief Commissioner at Scotland Yard. He authorizes me to request you to cooperate in any possible way with Agents Wright and Stevenson of the United States Drug Enforcement Agency during their current investigations in Tampica.

Please remember me to Mrs. Tibbett. Alice and I hope you will both revisit the Seawards before too long.

Sincerely,
Alfred Pendleton

Henry grinned. "You thought of everything."

Wright grinned back. "I had to. You were being a damned nuisance."

"You haven't yet told me how you found out who I really was."

Wright swirled his drink slowly. "No. And I don't think I will. I don't want to cause trouble for—well, let's leave it at that." He sipped his drink. "Who put you up to this crazy one-man act, anyway?"

"Sir Edward Ironmonger and a remarkable old lady called Lucy Pontefract-Deacon. I believe you've met her."

"Once. She didn't approve of me. That was what I intended, of course. I think I would probably trust her."

Henry said, "You seem to be implying that you wouldn't trust Sir Edward."

"I don't trust anybody connected with this government. It's as simple as that."

Henry let this pass. He said, "There's another thing. You were supposed to lure Carruthers and his people onto *Bellissima*, which is American territory—and arrest them there. I can't do that."

"Of course you can't. But you can get them to the British Seawards and make your arrest, with the Governor's cooperation."

"I suppose I might be able to. But how?"

"Up to you, old man." Wright had assumed a faint mock-British accent.

Henry glared at him, but all he said was, "The first problem is what to do with poor Agent Stevenson. The hotel management has of course discovered that he gave a false address. They are naturally very anxious to trace his next of kin."

"I'll take care of that," Wright promised. "There's bound to be an inquest, and so on, but I hope they'll let me send poor old Ernie back to his family in the States. Meanwhile, there are more urgent things to settle. Once I leave this cottage, I can't have any more contact with you in Tampica. It was risky enough coming here, except that I hope that if I was noticed, it will be thought that I came to threaten you. Which is why you will fly to the Seawards this afternoon. I can be there in *Bellissima* by tomorrow morning. We'll meet at Government House. We can talk there."

Henry stood up. "Here, wait a minute. What about my wife?"

"It's better if you come alone. Put her into cold storage

110

somewhere, without telling her anything. And I mean anything."

"I can't possibly do that."

"Of course you can. Tell her that I'm threatening to revenge myself on you through her, and that she must leave Pirate's Cave."

Henry smiled. "I've tried that. It only made her more determined to stay. Anyhow, I don't intend to start lying to her."

"I'm afraid you'll have to, old fellow." The scornful British intonation was more marked. "This isn't a jolly old game of cricket, you know. It's serious."

"I know it is. But—"

"Why don't you send her to stay with the old girl at Sugar Mill House? Make some excuse. Tell her you have to go to the Seawards, if you must. But don't tell her why."

Henry said, "I think that Sir Edward Ironmonger is in the Seawards. I could say I have to go and see him—"

"Is he?" Wright smiled sardonically. "I find that interesting." He stood up. "I'll go and see the hotel manager now, and then I'll be on my way. See you tomorrow."

"You'll find Bishop a good man to deal with," Henry said.

Wright paused at the door. "You trust too many people, Tibbett. In this matter, you'll trust nobody. Not even your wife."

He went out quickly, closing the door behind him.

9

At Sugar Mill House, Emmy was saying, "Look here, Lucy—I must go back, even if it's only to tell Henry where I am and collect some clothes. Since you won't telephone—"

"I have no intention," said Lucy, "of announcing your whereabouts to anybody on the telephone. However, I do take your point. Henry must be told. I shall go over to Pirate's Cave. It will give me something to do."

"How will you get there?"

"Samuel's mother has a car. She often drives me over the mountain." Lucy rang the little silver bell, which instantly produced Samuel.

"Yes, Miz Lucy?"

"Samuel, run along and ask Miss Ella if she would drive me to Tampica Harbour right away, will you? Tell her I'm in a hurry."

"Yes, Miz Lucy.'

"And while I'm gone, get some lunch for Mrs. Tibbett. Will a salad do you, Emmy?"

"Of course."

"Samuel makes a most excellent lobster salad." Lucy beamed at the young man. "I leave you in good hands. I shall be back this afternoon."

Henry was beginning to get hungry for his lunch. He was also slightly worried about Emmy and was considering whether it would be safe to telephone Sugar Mill House, when there was a tap on his door. Without waiting for him to open it, Lucy walked in.

"Lucy! What are you doing here? Have you seen Emmy?"

"I certainly have." Lucy closed the door behind her. "She is at my house, and she is going to stay there, at least for a while. I've come to pack a suitcase for her."

Henry went up and kissed the old lady on both cheeks.

"Lucy, you're a miracle. Nothing I could say would persuade her to leave Pirate's Cave—but you did it on your head. I'm so glad. Especially as I have to go away for a day or so."

"Go away? Where to?"

Henry hesitated. "Sir Edward is in the Seaward Islands."

"I know he is, drat him." Lucy grimaced.

"We can meet there and talk freely. It's impossible to get anything done here when it's so difficult to communicate."

Lucy looked at him quizzically. She said, "Show me where Emmy's things are, and I'll pack a small suitcase for her." She began sorting through the contents of Emmy's clothes' drawers. "I see *Bellissima* is back."

"Correct."

"How do you think Brinkman's death will affect De Marco's plans?"

"I hope it will persuade him to clear out of here," Henry said.

Lucy considered. "If it does, it will mean that we've failed. We shall just have to wait for the next approach, and try to

113

trap those crooks on our own. You can hardly stay on here indefinitely. It's all a great nuisance. Let's just hope that De Marco decides to go ahead with the deal by himself. In which case, it would surely be foolish of you to go off-island, even to consult with Eddie."

Henry thought for a moment. Then he said, "Lucy—can you keep a secret?"

Lucy bridled. "How can you possibly ask such a thing?"

Henry grinned at her. "Well, be sure to keep this one. The fact is, I've had a message from the Governor of the Seawards. He wants me to go there for a consultation with himself and Sir Edward."

With a little snort of skepticism, Lucy said, "Really? How very singular. How does Alfred Pendleton come into this, if I may ask?"

"I'll find that out," said Henry blandly, "when I get there."

"And how did this extraordinary message reach you?"

"It was brought personally by a member of the Governor's staff. He flew in this morning and has gone back already."

"What was his name? I know most of the Seawards people."

Henry said, "He didn't tell me his name. He showed me the message, and I recognized Sir Alfred's signature. He wouldn't even leave the letter with me. So you see what I mean about keeping it secret."

Lucy sniffed. "It's the most peculiar thing I ever heard. How do you know it's genuine? You may be walking into a trap."

"I told you, Lucy. I know Sir Alfred's signature—"

Lucy sailed on, ignoring the interruption. "Or at best, somebody is getting you out of the way while the drug negotiations are concluded. I think you'd be mad to leave here."

Henry decided that the conversation must stop. "Well, I'm going."

"And what on earth will Emmy think? What am I to say to her?"

Quickly, Henry said, "You can tell her I've gone to the Seawards. No more."

Lucy's eyebrows went up. "Goodness me. I thought you two had no secrets from each other."

"Normally we don't. You know that. But this is a very special—"

"—piece of idiocy." Lucy finished the sentence for him. She snapped the suitcase shut. "Well, if I can't stop you, I can't stop you. I'll just say this. Pretty silly you and Eddie will both feel if you come back and you find *Bellissima* gone and the deal concluded and not a shred of hard evidence against Carruthers and Palmer. We may not get another chance like this in years. By the way," she added, as an afterthought, "who killed Brinkman?"

"Opinions vary. Dolphin thinks it was an obeah-man."

Lucy snorted. Henry went on, "Well, he swears he saw somebody on the beach early this morning. A small man. He added a whole lot of rubbish about blood on the man's hands and feet. However, I do think that he probably caught a glimpse of whoever sabotaged the boat."

"And who was that?" Lucy spoke sharply.

"I'm afraid I don't know."

"Well, you should."

"Do you know, Lucy?"

Tartly, the old lady replied, "I was off-island, and in any case it's not my province. You are the detective."

This appeared to be her exit line, but at the door she turned and said, "Take care, Henry. Good luck." And with a brilliant smile, she was gone.

——

After he had had his lunch, Henry went in search of Patrick Bishop. As the secretary ushered him into the manager's office, the telephone rang. Bishop motioned Henry to sit down, while he answered it.

"Bishop here . . . Ah, yes, Brian . . . Good of you to call back . . . Oh, that's splendid, works out very well . . . Yes, for a couple of weeks . . . It'll be the best possible thing for him . . . Thanks, old man . . ." He hung up and turned to Henry. "That was the Secretary of the Golf Club on St. Matthews, in the Seawards. You know it?"

"By repute," said Henry, "as the most expensive and exclusive resort in the Caribbean."

"Yes." Bishop smiled. "It's even more outrageous than we are. However, Brian had some good news. Their parasailing boatman is due for a couple of weeks leave, and I've arranged for him to borrow Dolphin."

"You've seen Dolphin? How is he?"

"It's quite remarkable," said Bishop. "He's pulled himself together extraordinarily well." He gave Henry an amused glance. "I gather his recovery was not unconnected with yourself. Anyhow, he came to see me and said he'd like to go on with his job. Well, of course, our boat is out of action—and anyhow, after the accident, I think it's better to suspend parasailing for a bit. So it's a remarkable piece of luck that Dolphin can work at the Golf Club. Best thing for him—like remounting at once after you've fallen off a horse. Anyhow, that's not what you wanted to see me about. Is Lucy back?"

"Yes," said Henry. "She just went to the Seawards for a short visit. What I wanted to tell you is that my wife and I will be spending a few days off-island."

Bishop nodded approvingly. "Very sensible. See a bit more of the region while you're here."

"That's right. Can we keep on our cottage while we're away and leave some of our things there?"

"No problem, Mr. Tibbett. No problem. Have a pleasant trip."

By the time Henry left Pirate's Cave by taxi bound for the airport, *Bellissima* had upped anchor and departed. It occurred to Henry that a boat of her size and power would not take many hours to reach the Seawards—a journey that only took thirty minutes by small aircraft. However, if Wright was in a hurry to be off, that was his business.

The elegant sixteen-seater Otter took off gracefully, a lightweight among the big jets coming in and out of Tampica airport, and a moment later Henry was looking down on Sugar Mill House, where he could see Emmy's hired Jeep parked in the driveway. He felt a pang of guilt. On some other cases in which Emmy had been involved, he had kept certain bits of dangerous information from her, for her own protection, but he had never deliberately lied to her. He thought of Wright, and his thoughts were less than friendly.

The territory known as the British Seaward Islands comprises as many as fifteen islands, most of them piously named after Christian saints by their discoverer, Columbus. However, most are not more than a knoll of scrub breaking the brilliant surface of the Caribbean. Visiting yachts can be seen anchored off their white coral beaches, but if there is any human habitation it takes the form of a small beach bar, which is locked up and deserted at sundown, when the owner makes his way by boat back to his village. This will be on either St. Mark's or St. Matthew's, the two inhabited islands. St. Mark's is the larger of the two, the administrative center of the group. Here are Government House, the Legislative Building, the hospital, and the airport.

Most of Henry's friends on the Seawards lived on the smaller island of St. Matthew's, and he felt glad of this, for he had no desire to broadcast his presence in the territory. He took a taxi from the airport straight to Government House—a pretty, lightweight confection of sugar-icing arches and shady balconies dating from the eighteenth century. He was ushered into a big, cool drawing room with sweeping views over the sea. As he came in, two men got up from the Victorian armchairs in which they had been sitting—a slightly built Englishman with a thin, intellectual face, and a large, powerful black man. His Excellency the Governor, Sir Alfred Pendleton, and the Governor-General of Tampica, Sir Edward Ironmonger.

"Good to see you, Tibbett," said Sir Alfred. "Take a pew. You know Ironmonger, of course."

"Of course," said Henry. He smiled at Sir Edward and was rewarded by a huge grin.

The Governor went on. "What brings you to the Seawards, Chief Superintendent?"

"To be frank," said Henry, unhappily aware that he was being just the opposite, "I came in the hope of finding Eddie here." It was the first time that he had used Ironmonger's informal Christian name. "I wasn't sure if he had heard about Brinkman's death."

"It was on the radio," said Pendleton.

"Did they give any details?" Henry asked.

"A parasailing accident. Nothing more." Sir Alfred smiled. "Come and sit down, Mr. Tibbett, and tell me why you are interested in the late Mr. Brinkman."

Knowing as he did that the Governor was well aware of Brinkman's real identity, Henry realized that this was a

118

sledgehammer of a hint. Not a word to Eddie. More deception. He sat down.

"You don't know, Sir Alfred? I thought Eddie might have told you."

"I was just about to," put in Ironmonger. "I've been trying to see Alfred all day, but—"

"I'm afraid my schedule was very busy," said Pendleton smoothly. "I do apologize, Eddie. Perhaps you'll tell me now."

Another hint. Let him tell his own story.

Ironmonger said, "Bluntly, Alfred, we think—in fact, we know"—he gave Henry a conspiratorial smile—"that Brinkman and his colleague De Marco were Mafia agents about to put through a big drug deal with several high-ranking Tampican officials."

The Governor interrupted. "You say 'we.' Who else was suspicious?"

"Lucy Pontefract-Deacon, of course. It was she who went over to London and persuaded Tibbett to come and help us get the evidence we needed. It almost looked as if we had succeeded. The deal was to have been clinched on board De Marco's yacht, *Bellissima*, within the next few days. Now, of course, Brinkman's death has changed everything. I imagine De Marco will abort his plan and go back to the States for instructions." Sir Edward produced his inevitable cigar. "Do you mind?" Sir Alfred shook his head and Ironmonger lit up. "However, that's not really important. What matters is that Tibbett has the evidence we need."

"Just a moment, Eddie." Henry sat forward in his chair. "I don't understand this. What made you think that the deal was about to go through?"

Ironmonger did a slight double-take, and removed the cigar from his mouth. "My dear Henry, I received your message."

"I sent you no message."

"You didn't?"

"I called your special number this morning and was told you were off-island, probably in the Seawards. I certainly left no message."

Smiling wryly, Pendleton said, "There appears to be some confusion somewhere."

"You're damn right there is." Henry was angry. He turned to Ironmonger. "What message was I supposed to have left for you?"

Without hesitation, Sir Edward replied, " 'Mission successful. Final meeting Friday. Meet me Seawards Wednesday to discuss. Scott.' "

"Melinda gave you that message?"

"She did. She said it was phoned through by a white man."

"When?"

"Early this morning. Naturally, I took the first plane."

"Was the caller British or American?"

"I'm afraid Melinda wouldn't be able to distinguish, any more than you could tell if I was from Tampica or Barbados."

Henry said, "She must have thought I was crazy, calling again about an hour later and asking for you."

Sir Edward said, "Melinda is very discreet and just takes messages. If she thought about it at all, I expect she imagined that you were checking up to make sure I had got the message and was on my way to the Seawards."

Henry said, "Well, here's the truth. Not only did I leave no message, but my mission was far from successful." To Pendleton, he explained, "I intercepted a message which set a rendezvous on *Bellissima* yesterday evening. Eddie gave lunch to De Marco and his crewman, getting them off the boat so that I could plant a recording device on board.

Voice-activated. We hoped to get a tape of the meeting, which I would recover later."

"So what happened, Henry?" Sir Edward sounded bleak.

"What happened was that De Marco found my device as soon as he got back to the boat. He used it to record a message threatening my life and Emmy's if we didn't keep our noses out of his business. He also said that there had been no rendezvous, that the whole thing had been set up to trap us. I tried to tell you yesterday evening, but the market was closed and there was no reply. And this morning I was told you were off-island."

"So there is no evidence after all." Sir Edward spoke quietly, but his fury was obvious. "I see. That would seem to put us back to square one, as they say. Or perhaps square minus one. I'm afraid your time has been wasted, Chief Superintendent. And Lucy's. And mine."

"Not entirely." Pendleton sounded faintly amused. "You have evidence against De Marco on Mr. Tibbett's tape, if he issued threats."

"That's quite beside the point, Alfred."

"I don't think so, Eddie," said the Governor. "As far as De Marco is concerned, he must think his threats have worked. Mr. Tibbett has left Tampica." He turned to Henry. "Is your wife with you here in the Seawards?"

"No," said Henry, "but she's not at Pirate's Cave either. She's . . ." He hesitated a moment, and then decided that Wright's suspicions of Ironmonger were ridiculous. "She's staying with Lucy at Sugar Mill House."

"Good. Good. So you see, Eddie," said Sir Alfred, "there's really no reason why De Marco shouldn't carry on as planned. I think you should go back to Tampica and pursue your inquiries. For the moment, Mr. Tibbett will stay here, and I think Mrs. Tibbett should join him."

"This is not at all the way I planned this operation." Sir Edward was making a great effort to control himself, but Henry could tell the depth of his feelings by the fact that his English had become suddenly stilted. "I shall, of course, return to Tampica at once." He looked at his watch. "It is just after four o'clock. I can catch the four-thirty plane, and I shall drive to Sugar Mill House to fetch Mrs. Tibbett. She can come here on the seven-fifteen. Then Lucy and I will, as I said, start again from square minus one. Mr. Tibbett's activities seem to have done us more harm than good." He stood up. "Goodbye, Alfred."

When the door had closed behind Ironmonger, Pendleton passed a hand over his forehead. "Phew," he said. "Sorry about that, Tibbett. Parting brass rags with Eddie, I mean. It seemed to be the only way."

Henry said, "Agent Wright seems to think that even Sir Edward—"

"I know he does. I don't agree with him, but he's a highly trained professional and I respect his opinion. I gather he'll be here tomorrow morning."

"So I understand. Or even sooner. *Bellissima* is a fast boat."

"Stevenson's death is a complication. Do you know who killed him?"

Henry shook his head. "No. Nor do I know who telephoned that message to Ironmonger—except that it was somebody who used my code name, which I thought only my wife knew."

"If there really was a message," said Pendleton, thoughtfully. "Ironmonger could have invented it. Or the person called Melinda. Who is she?"

"I've no idea," said Henry. "I only know she runs a shop in Tampica Harbour. Her name is Murphy—like about a thousand other people on Tampica. Sir Edward trusts her implicitly to take messages for him. I've only spoken to her on the phone."

"Well, I daresay you'll be able to sort out that small mystery. Meanwhile, you must tell me what brings you here."

"Didn't Wright explain?"

"He could hardly have done so over an open radio channel. He simply let me know that he would be arriving himself. I presume it has to do with Stevenson's death."

"Of course. Wright feels that his cover has been well and truly blown."

"Surely anybody can have an accident parasailing."

"This wasn't an accident. The boat was sabotaged."

"Stevenson might well have survived," Pendleton pointed out.

"I know," said Henry. "This was meant as a warning. Somebody on Tampica knew that Wright and Stevenson were DEA agents, and intended to scare them off."

"Any idea who?"

Henry shook his head. "Someone in the government, is my guess."

"So what does Wright want you to do now? I presume you've discussed the situation with him."

Glumly, Henry said, "He wants me to take over where he and Stevenson left off. Posing as a rival drug runner. I'm supposed to lure the Tampican gang over here, where they can be arrested under British law. The details are to be worked out when he arrives tomorrow."

"I see." Pendleton thought for a moment. "Then I think we must conclude that you arranged the mishap to the towboat."

Henry sat up straight. "Now, wait a minute—"

"Just let us suppose," continued Sir Alfred, "that you really are a drug trafficker. You have been briefed that Tampica is an excellent staging post, and that some high government officials are eminently bribable. You are furnished with the identity of a rich, retired British businessman, accompanied by his wife. You arrive on the island—and what do you find?"

Henry nodded. "Competition. A team of two."

"You report the fact to your masters. Their news is alarming. Nobody has ever heard of De Marco, Brinkman, or the *Bellissima*. At best, they are amateurs; at worst, they are DEA."

"Of course," said Henry. "At all costs, I have to get rid of them. An accident which can quite easily be proved to have been sabotage is an ingenious idea." He smiled. "I wonder if certain people will remember that if I hadn't made such a fuss the boat would have broken up on the reef, and the damaged steering gear might never have been discovered."

Pendleton said, "You were ideally situated to get at the boat, staying at Pirate's Cave."

"In a cottage right on the beach," Henry agreed. "The boatman thinks he saw a slightly built man running off into the trees early that morning. It could easily have been me." He added, "I suppose you see where this is leading us?"

"To a very credible story to spin to the Tampicans."

"I wasn't thinking of that, sir. I was thinking that there may very likely be another potential drug runner on the island."

10

The 7:15 flight from Tampica touched down in St. Mark's at 8:20—only just over half an hour late, which is good by Caribbean timing. Henry saw the lights of the small plane coming in from his perch on the deserted rooftop observation platform, and quickly went downstairs and stationed himself by the exit door from the Customs area.

Before too long, passengers began coming through—first those with only hand baggage, then a small stream of people with suitcases, most of them clearly tourists, about ten in all. As the swing door opened for the last time, Henry could see that the inspection bench was deserted, and that the Customs officer was going back into his office. The last passenger was through, and there was no sign of Emmy.

Trying to suppress the first tinglings of alarm, Henry went to the desk of the British Seaward Airways, where the pilot was checking in with a clerk. Everybody else seemed to have gone home.

"No, sir, the flight was not full. No, sir, no other flight tonight from Tampica. Next one arrives at seven-forty tomorrow morning."

There was no point in hanging around the airport. Henry went back to the car Alfred Pendleton had lent him, and drove back to Government House. He told himself that there was no need to panic. Sir Edward's flight must have been late in getting to Tampica—weren't nearly all Caribbean planes late—and he had not been able to get to Sugar Mill House in time for Emmy to catch the seven-fifteen. It was annoying, but not serious. Emmy would arrive on the first flight in the morning.

Pendleton was waiting in the hall to greet him. It had been arranged that dinner should be postponed until Emmy's arrival. He came up, all smiles.

"Ah, Tibbett. Not too late, considering." A pause. "Where's Mrs. Tibbett?"

"She wasn't on the plane. She must be coming tomorrow morning instead. Sorry about dinner."

Sir Alfred looked nonplussed. "But—she *was* on the plane. Lucy telephoned."

"She did?"

"Around six o'clock. Said that Mrs. Tibbett had had a lift to the airport and was catching the seven-fifteen."

"Oh, my God," said Henry. "And no message since?"

"Not a word."

"We'll have to call Lucy back, even if it is risky. Maybe something went wrong, and she didn't like to ring again—you know she's scared of wiretaps. You'd better do it, if you don't mind, sir. It wouldn't do for anybody to hear my voice."

"Of course. Come into my study."

As Sir Alfred dialed the Tampica number, Henry picked up the extension. After a couple of rings, Lucy's robust voice floated down the line.

"Sugar Mill House."

"Lucy, it's Alfred Pendleton."

"How are you, Alfred dear? Our friend arrived safely, I trust?"

126

"No, Lucy, she didn't."

"What?"

"She wasn't on the plane."

A little pause. "Now, don't be silly, Alfred. Of course she was on the plane. She left here with—with our mutual friend—at about five past six. In that big car, they'd have been at the airport soon after half past. She couldn't possibly have missed the flight."

Putting his hand over the mouthpiece of the telephone, Henry said to Pendleton, "Ask her about Emmy's Jeep."

Pendleton nodded. "What happened to her hired Jeep, Lucy?"

"It's still here. Barney's sending someone to collect it tomorrow. Meanwhile, where is she?"

"Exactly." Sir Alfred sounded grim. "You'll have to try to find her, Lucy. Try the hospital and the police."

"You realize, Alfred, that I hardly know the woman." Lucy had evidently remembered the possibility of bugging.

Sir Alfred winked at Henry. "I know that, Lucy, but I think it would be only civil to make inquiries about a missing person—even if she is only an acquaintance."

"Very well. I'll call back if I have any news. Good-bye, Alfred."

Henry put down his telephone. "I must get back to Tampica at once."

"My dear fellow, you can't. For one thing, there's no way of getting there before tomorrow morning. And in any case, you have a meeting here with Agent Wright."

"To hell with Agent Wright. Emmy may be in danger."

Soothingly, Pendleton said, "Now, sit down and have a drink, Tibbett. Lucy will do all that's humanly possible, and I really don't think that Emmy will come to any harm in Tampica."

"I can't think what leads you to that conclusion," said Henry. However, he did sit down and accept a whiskey.

"Well," said Pendleton, "look at it this way. Either Carruthers has rumbled you, or he hasn't. If he hasn't, then there's no reason for anybody to harm Emmy. There's probably a perfectly simple explanation and we'll soon know it. On the other hand, if he *has* rumbled you, then he'll be wanting to get both you and Emmy out of the country double-quick, before you get any solid evidence against him. The worst way to do that would be to abduct Emmy. Does that sound logical?"

"I suppose so."

"Then let's have something to eat."

Henry was glad that Lady Pendleton was away in England, because he felt in no mood for small talk. In fact, the soup plates had been removed and the roast beef not yet served, when the butler announced that Sir Alfred was wanted on the telephone. Long distance from Tampica.

"Alfred? Lucy. A most peculiar thing has happened."

"What? Have you found Mrs. Tibbett?"

"Yes and no."

"What does that mean?"

"I called the hospital first." Lucy was being maddeningly deliberate. "No news there. Then I managed to contact the person who drove her to the airport. He says he dropped her there with a good half hour to spare for the flight."

"Oh, do get on with it, Lucy."

"Then," said Lucy, "I telephoned the police. The duty sergeant said he'd never even heard of her. So that seemed to be that. Then, just a few minutes ago, I had a call from Commissioner Kelly himself. And he told me"—Lucy paused for dramatic effect—"he told me that Mrs. Tibbett was under arrest."

"*Under arrest?* What on earth for?"

"Irregularities in her documents. That's what he said."

"That's ridiculous!"

"I know it's ridiculous, Alfred dear. But Tampica is an independent state and has a perfect right to detain anybody whom it feels to be suspicious."

"Where is she? Can you see her? Has she got a lawyer?"

"Wait a minute, wait a minute. Naturally I asked all those questions. Kelly told me that she wasn't in jail."

"Well, that's something. She's back at Pirate's Cave, is she?"

Lucy paused. "Actually, no. All he would say is that she's under house arrest."

"In whose house, for God's sake?"

"Apparently she's been taken to the house of a high government official. It was unthinkable, Kelly said, that a lady of Mrs. Tibbett's distinction should be put in prison, but it was necessary for her to be detained. He said I couldn't see her."

"And what about a lawyer?"

"He just said very smoothly that it was being attended to."

Pendleton passed a hand over his forehead. "What high government official?"

"I should imagine," said Lucy, "that Mrs. Tibbett is either at Joe Palmer's house, or at The Lodge."

"The Lodge?"

"The Prime Minister's residence. Chez Carruthers, in fact." After a pause, Lucy went on, "What do we do now, Alfred?"

"We get on to the nearest British Consul," said Pendleton. "Where's that? Oh, Lord, in Barbados, bloody miles away.

Never mind—I'll telephone him and get him to call Tampica to say he's coming over. They'll have to let him see her."

"Surely I can do something?" Lucy protested.

"I don't think so, my dear."

"If you're trying to protect me—"

"Nothing of the sort." Sir Alfred was very firm. "You have been a great help—but after all, as you said, you hardly know Mrs. Tibbett. This must go through the proper channels."

"Damn and blast the proper channels!"

"Good-bye, Lucy." Pendleton put down the telephone and turned to Henry, who had been listening on the other line. "What do you make of that, Tibbett?"

"She's been kidnapped." Henry was very grim. "There couldn't possibly be anything wrong with Emmy's papers. They've taken her hostage."

Sir Alfred sighed. "I'm afraid you're right. Still, a call from the British Consul may make them think a bit. I'll ring him right away." He picked up the phone and began to dial.

Fortunately, the consul was at home, and he listened sympathetically to Sir Alfred's request. It might, however, he said, be a little difficult to intervene at this early stage. After all, Mrs. Tibbett would probably be free tomorrow. Pendleton must realize that some of these newly independent countries were a bit trigger-happy when it came to irregularities in tourists' papers, but things always got sorted out quite quickly. The worst they could do would be to deport her.

"Mrs. Tibbett's papers are perfectly in order." Sir Alfred seldom raised his voice, but he did so now. "And she is not an ordinary tourist—she is the wife of a high British official. What's more, she hasn't been detained by the police in the usual way. The police have never heard of her. She's been spirited off to the home of some government official. For heaven's sake, man—"

The consul was soothing. All right, all right, he would telephone in the morning and find out the facts of the case. Naturally, the woman's husband must be worried, but there was really no need for alarm. Good night, old man.

Pendleton's next call was to Sir Edward Ironmonger. Henry had protested against talking on an open line to the Governor-General, but Pendleton overruled him. Without mentioning Emmy's name, he asked Ironmonger whether their friend had caught the plane all right.

"To the best of my knowledge—yes." Sir Edward sounded far from pleased and still ruffled by the afternoon's unpleasantness. "No, I didn't go into the airport with her. I dropped her about a hundred yards from the entrance. I thought it prudent. Hasn't she arrived, then?"

"Not yet. You didn't see if she spoke to anyone or—"

"I've told you. I dropped her off and drove straight home. Do you want me to—?"

"No, no. Thanks, old man, but—no. Not at this stage. I'll keep in touch."

The night seemed endless and sleepless to Henry, although he did finally drop off for a couple of hours, and woke feeling guilty. Shortly after ten o'clock the next morning, the telephone rang.

The consul in Barbados sounded both puzzled and impatient. "Really, Sir Alfred, I can't make head nor tail of this business of Mrs. Tibbett."

"Why? What's happened?"

"Well, I telephoned this morning, as I promised. Asked to speak to the Commissioner of Police—chap called Kelly. His office told me he was out—up at a place called The Lodge, which is the Prime Minister's residence—for some sort of meeting. Anyway, they put me through there—it's all on the government switchboard—and finally I made contact with him. And he flatly denies it."

"Denies what?"

"That this Mrs. Tibbett of yours is in any kind of custody. He says he never made any call to that old woman, and that there was no question of papers being out of order. He said if somebody did make a call—which he doubts—it must have been a hoax. He strongly implied that the Pontefract-Deacon biddy is more than halfway round the bend. After all, she's ninety."

"Age has nothing to do with it," snapped Pendleton. "She's as sane as I am. Well, what did you do then?"

"On Kelly's advice," said the consul, "I then called British Seaward Airways in Tampica. It may or may not surprise you to hear that Mrs. Tibbett's name was on the manifest for yesterday evening's flight, and Immigration has her departure form, duly filled in and stamped. Moreover, the girl at the desk remembers checking her in, taking her baggage, and issuing her with a boarding card."

"Then where the hell is she?" Sir Alfred was exasperated.

"My dear chap, I've no idea. That's her business, don't you think? But wherever she is, she's not in Tampica. I'm afraid I can't do any more for you." The line went dead.

Henry and Pendleton stood looking at each other, each with a telephone in his hand. Before either could find words, the door opened and the Governor's secretary said, "Agent Wright of the Drug Enforcement Agency to see you, sir."

Wright strode into the study, hand outstretched.

"Good morning, Sir Alfred. Hi, there, Tibbett. Sorry I couldn't make it earlier. The sea was—" He stopped, looking at the faces of the two men. "Hey, what goes on here? You look like you've seen a ghost."

Sir Alfred pulled himself together. "Sit down, Wright. I'll explain."

Wright listened in silence. Then he said, "So you think they've snatched Mrs. Tibbett."

"There's no other possible explanation," said Henry.

"Why the hell didn't you leave her where she was, at Sugar Mill House?" Wright was angry. "I knew she'd only complicate things."

"We didn't think she was safe on Tampica—not after Ironmonger's curious account of getting a faked message from me. We seem to have been proved right." Henry glared at the DEA agent.

Pendleton poured oil on troubled waters. He advanced his theory that there might be another would-be drug runner on the island, who saw the Tibbetts as rivals. "She's probably safer with the Tampican government villains," he ended. "But the puzzling thing is—why? What do they hope to get out of it?"

"Money," said Wright, laconically. "My guess is you'll be hearing from them before long."

"I still don't—"

Wright put his outspread hands on the table and leaned forward. "See here, let me tell you just how far we'd gotten when Ernie was killed." He paused. "Better begin at the beginning. We turned up on *Bellissima* with quite a group of guys and girls—all agents posing as vacationers. Very popular assignment, that was. We'd taken care to visit other islands on the way—just a bunch of yuppies on a Caribbean cruise. We dropped Ernie off in Tampica with the story that he got seasick and wanted to stay ashore. He was an experienced parasailor, and he took it up with great enthusiasm. Came in very useful. All these government guys live in houses up the hillside from the beach, and he was able to get a bird's-eye view. See who got together in whose houses, and so on. He soon realized that Carruthers and Palmer were thick as thieves. So that was where he started."

"He made contact with Carruthers?" Henry asked.

"Not at first. Joe Palmer was the man. Ernie put out a spiel about wanting to invest in the island. That soon got to Joe's ears."

"How?" said Henry.

Wright looked surprised. "I don't know exactly how. You know how the bush telegraph works on these islands. Ernie talked about it at the hotel—"

"And somebody at the hotel passed it on to Palmer. Any idea who?"

"None at all. Could have been a waiter, a maid—"

"Or the manager," said Henry flatly.

Wright shrugged. "Or the manager, as you say. What does it matter? The point is that Palmer approached Ernie, gave him a tour of the island, invited him to lunch, suggested he meet Carruthers."

"This sounds familiar," said Henry. "I was given the same treatment."

"Ah, but you didn't give the right answers."

"Right answers?"

"The unwritten code is that you say you think Tampica has big potential, if only they can find the right investors. It's like a Masonic handshake. Nothing has been said, but everybody knows where they stand."

"The right investors." Henry frowned. "I seem to remember saying just that."

"You did?"

"Yes, I'm sure that's what I said. I was just trying to avoid being drawn into a discussion of anything definite."

Wright leaned back in his chair and laughed. "Mr. Tibbett, you're a genius. From that moment on, whether you knew it or not, you were regarded as a dealer. This should make your job a lot easier."

"We'll see about that," said Henry.

Wright went on. "The two who were definitely interested in Ernie's proposals were Carruthers and Palmer. Everything was said in oblique double-talk, but the two of them had gotten as far as agreeing in principle to come aboard *Bellissima* to discuss investment in the island. Ernie mentioned a million dollars. Palmer said that the last group of really suitable investors had come up with a million and a half. Ernie replied that the actual sum he could offer would depend on the exact facilities that his investment would ensure him. At that Carruthers intervened, shut Palmer up like a clam, and said that such matters could only be talked about in complete privacy. That's when Ernie suggested *Bellissima*."

Henry said, "What about Kelly?"

Wright rubbed his chin. "Ernie wasn't too sure. A deal like this would pretty well have to have the cooperation of the police, but Kelly didn't appear as a principal. Ernie fancied he might be wanting out, but didn't dare say so."

"Sir Edward Ironmonger?" It was Pendleton who put the question.

"Once again, no direct involvement—and if Tibbett is right, he's trying to break the thing up. Ostensibly, at least."

"Ironmonger has nothing to do with it." Henry was indignant. "He loves Tampica and he's determined to smash the drug trade."

Wright and Pendleton exchanged a glance. Then Wright

135

said, "I've already warned Mr. Tibbett about too much simple faith. The same argument applies to Ironmonger as to Kelly. It would be difficult to operate on that scale without the knowledge of the Governor-General. I'm not about to start trusting him unconditionally. However, to get on. Two days before Ernie's death, a rather odd thing happened."

"What was that?"

"He was approached by Mrs. Carruthers—the beautiful Carmelita. Unlike her husband and Palmer, she was anything but discreet. She asked him straight out to supply her with cocaine—her beloved white girl."

"Good Lord," said Henry. "Why?"

"Presumably because she needed it."

"She could surely get as much as she wanted on Tampica."

"I don't think so," said Wright. "Her position is delicate, to say the least. My own guess is that her husband doesn't know about her habit and would be very angry if he found out. The people who make money from drugs are usually not addicts themselves, and it would be fatal for Carruthers if cocaine was traced to his wife."

Henry said, "What did Stevenson do? Give it to her?"

"No. Quite apart from the fact that DEA isn't in the drug-pushing business, he didn't have any to hand out. He promised to try to arrange for a supply."

"I should have thought," said Pendleton, "that as part of your disguise as drug runners, you'd at least have brought a sample along."

"You don't understand." Wright was patient. "We weren't posing as pushers trying to sell the white girl in Tampica. We made ourselves out to be much more important than that. We represented multimillion-dollar interests, and what we wanted was to use Tampica as a halfway house for contraband between South America and the United States. People of that standing don't carry drugs around like traveling salesmen."

"So—was she satisfied?"

"Addicts," said Wright, "are never satisfied except with a fix. All I can tell you is that she promptly went off-island, presumably looking for a fix. As a matter of fact"—Wright looked hard at Sir Alfred—"as a matter of fact, she came here."

Pendleton raised his hands, hopelessly. "I wish I could say that she couldn't possibly have got it here. I hope she couldn't—but I can't be sure."

"Well, as far as I know she hasn't come back to Tampica. Maybe she's gone further afield. It doesn't really concern me—except for one thing."

"What's that?" Henry asked.

"It's just possible," said Wright, "that Ernie's failure to come up with any coke made her suspicious. Carruthers's previous associates may have been more forthcoming. I have a sort of feeling that it was Carmelita who pulled the chain on us before she left Tampica. However, none of that is really important. What is important is to map out your plan of campaign."

"What is important," said Henry, "is to find my wife."

"My dear fellow," Wright dropped into the mock-English accent that had irritated Henry before, "I really can't agree."

Henry turned to Pendleton. "Sir Alfred, you must help me."

The Governor shrugged. "I'd like to, of course, Tibbett, but I don't see what more I can do. You heard what the consul said. Tampica is a sovereign state, and we can't possibly interfere. I think the best thing you can do is to cooperate with Officer Wright's plans, go back to Tampica yourself—and see what you can do there."

11

Emmy woke up slowly, at first only vaguely aware of a bright light troubling her eyes. Her head ached and her mouth felt dry. Instinctively, she turned over to avoid the light, burying her face in the pillow. She was drifting off to sleep again when she noticed a strange smell. It wasn't an unpleasant smell, just an unfamiliar one: spicy and peppery, with undertones of fish and vinegar; the smell of West Indian cooking. Suddenly, she was awake. She turned onto her back again, and sat up.

She was in a bedroom that she had never seen before. The light that had hurt her eyes was sunlight streaming through an open window, and she could see purple bougainvillea blossoms peeping inquisitively around the white window frame. The room was furnished neatly but very simply—a bed, a table, a chair, a white-painted wardrobe, wooden floor with a woven rush mat. The cooking smell was drifting in through the window, and far away came the noise of pots and pans clanking, and a low murmur of voices—the sounds of a kitchen.

Pulling herself together, Emmy tried to remember the previous day. She had been at Sugar Mill House with Lucy—but this was not Sugar Mill House, or anything like it. Lucy had driven to Pirate's Cave to see Henry; and had come back with the news that Henry was going to the British Seawards and that she, Emmy, was to stay put with Lucy.

Then . . . something else had happened. What? Emmy frowned. Something to do with Sir Edward Ironmonger. That's right. Ironmonger had turned up at Sugar Mill House in the evening, driving one of those big black limousines, and he had said . . . Emmy beat her fists together in frustration, as her brain refused to disgorge the necessary information. Suddenly, it came. He had said that she was to join Henry on St. Mark's, and that he would drive her to the airport to catch the last plane. She had packed a suitcase.

Shakily, Emmy got out of bed and realized that she was still wearing her underclothes. Just her dress had been removed, and when she opened the wardrobe she saw it hanging neatly there. Beneath it was her suitcase, apparently unopened.

So, she ought to be with Henry now, in St. Mark's. But what about the journey? Why couldn't she remember? Where was Henry?

Emmy made her way to the open window. She was in an upper room of a house set on a high hill, with gardens tumbling colorfully down toward the sea, and the red and green rooftops of—yes, Tampica Harbour. No doubt about it. She could see the toylike boats in the harbor and even the distant sweep of Barracuda Bay, with its huge new hotels.

She went back to the bed again and sat down, cudgeling her memory. Sir Edward had driven her over the mountain to the airport. Yes, she remembered now, he had dropped her some way from the entrance, saying that it was wiser for him not to be seen with her. She had gone in and registered at the British Seaward Airways desk for the flight to St. Mark's. And then—nothing. A tiny glimmer of recollection—somebody calling her name. No more.

Well, Emmy decided, she had to get out of here, and fast. There seemed to be no visible means of washing in the room, so she put on her dress and brought her sponge-bag out of her case, which did indeed seem undisturbed. She ran a comb through her hair, and went to the door, hoping to find a bathroom. The door was locked.

At least the window is open, Emmy thought. She went over to it, noticing as she passed her suitcase that it still had attached to its handle a bright green tag with the black letters STM on it, which she recognized as the airline's designation for St. Mark's. So she had actually checked her baggage in, and it had been removed from the baggage cart before the aircraft was loaded. Curiouser and curiouser. She leaned out of the window.

Immediately below her, screened from the gardens by a palm-frond fence, was an enclosure with several big garbage bins; a few small hens picked about listlessly on the loose earth, and a black-and-white cat was washing itself with feline thoroughness and attention to detail. This must be the backyard of the house, and the spicy cooking smells obviously came from the kitchen, two stories down on the ground floor. There were no human beings in sight.

Emmy called out. "Hey! Somebody down there!"

The hens continued to pick, the cat continued to wash. There was no other sign of life. She called again, louder. "Hey! Somebody!"

The sound of a key turning in the door behind her sent her spinning around to face the room again. The door opened slowly, and an elderly, stout black woman came in. Emmy had never seen her before.

140

"Now, look here," Emmy began, "what on earth is going on? Where—?"

The woman folded her arms and looked at Emmy with no expression whatsoever. She said, "Come."

"Come where? I don't—"

The woman turned her back on Emmy and walked out into the passage. There seemed nothing to do but to follow. There was a door on the other side of the corridor, and this the black woman opened, revealing a bathroom. Then she turned, took Emmy's arm in a strong grip, and propelled her inside. At once the door closed and the key turned.

The bathroom was far from luxurious, but it had a shower, wash basin, and toilet, and quite an impressive array of towels and strongly scented soap. There was a new toothbrush, still in its cellophane wrapper, and an unopened tube of tooth-paste.

Emmy shrugged. No sense in not making use of the bathroom. She took a shower and felt a lot better, though no less baffled. When she had dressed again, she banged on the door. The key turned at once, the door opened, and the wardress—as Emmy was beginning to think of her—ushered her back into the bedroom.

The room had changed in two respects. First, and most noticeable, the window was now closed by two sturdy wooden shutters, firmly padlocked, and the electric light was on. Second, a tray bearing an appetizing breakfast had been placed on the table.

Emmy exploded. "This is beyond a joke! For heaven's sake, where am I? I demand to see the master of the house. I—"

She was talking to herself. The black woman had disappeared, locking the door behind her.

Feeling more and more like Alice in Wonderland, Emmy ate the breakfast, swallowing down two aspirins from her sponge-bag with the first cup of coffee. Soon her headache cleared, and she felt almost back to normal. She went over to the door, banged loudly on it, and rattled the handle. It had occurred to her that if her jailer was on duty outside, she might come to collect the tray, which would entail leaving the door open at some stage. With the tray in her hands, the black woman would be hampered, to say the least. Emmy thought she might have a hope of breaking out and running for it. However, nothing happened.

When the door finally did open again, it was to admit Chester Carruthers, the Prime Minister of Tampica. He was followed by the wardress, who shut and locked the door behind him and stood against it, arms folded.

Carruthers was wearing white cotton slacks and a loose, colorfully printed shirt. He looked very relaxed as he advanced, hand outstretched, smiling professionally.

"Good morning, Mrs. Tibbett. I trust you slept well, and that Annamabel is looking after you. I see you have enjoyed your breakfast."

Emmy ignored the proffered hand. "I slept well, as you call it, Mr. Carruthers, because I was doped. I ate my breakfast, but you can hardly imagine that I enjoyed it. Will you please tell me exactly where I am and what is going on?"

Carruthers raised his eyebrows. "Why, you are at The Lodge, Mrs. Tibbett. As my guest."

"Do you always lock your guests into their rooms?"

The smile deepened slightly. "Not always, Mrs. Tibbett. Only when it seems the prudent thing to do." Carruthers turned to the black woman. "Please wait outside, Annamabel. Lock the door behind you. I have a spare key."

Silently, Annamabel did as she was told. Carruthers sat down on the bed. "Now, Mrs. Tibbett, we can have a little talk."

"Oh, no, we can't. I demand to see the British Consul."

"The nearest British Consul is in Barbados, Mrs. Tibbett. And since your departure from Tampica is fully documented, I doubt if he would take such a request seriously. Do you mind if I smoke?"

Without waiting for a reply, Carruthers lit a small cigar. When he was satisfied that it was drawing, he said, "I must tell you, Mrs. Tibbett, that we know all about your husband, Mr. Henry Tibbett, the so-called retired businessman. We know that he has by no means retired." He puffed at his cigar. "What is he doing in the Seawards, by the way?"

Emmy was tongue-tied. What could she say? How much did Carruthers really know? He was looking at her quizzically. "Well, Mrs. Tibbett?"

Praying for guidance, Emmy said, "He . . . he had received a threat. . . ."

"From the charming Mr. De Marco, no doubt."

"Well . . . I don't really know. He couldn't imagine why anybody should be trying to run him off Tampica, but—well, he thought it would be a good idea to leave the island for a while."

Carruthers studied the end of his cigar. "Yes," he said. "Yes, I can see that. It was also a good idea to dispose of Brinkman, or whatever his name really was. Officers of the Drug Enforcement Agency are not exactly welcome on Tampica—are they, Mrs. Tibbett?"

The remark baffled Emmy completely. She started to say, "Henry's not—" and then stopped.

"Of course he's not," said Carruthers, easily. "Please don't

143

think that I was implying anything so unpleasant." He puffed at the cigar again. "I'll be frank with you, Mrs. Tibbett."

"That'll be a change."

Carruthers ignored this remark and went on smoothly. "I think we can do business with your husband. I hope we can. However, after recent events, we considered that it would be wise to have a little . . . a little insurance, as it were. That is why you are here."

Hopelessly out of her depth, Emmy tried to look intelligent. "I see," she said.

"Good. When may we expect to see Mr. Tibbett back in Tampica?"

This Emmy could answer. "I have no idea. As you must know, I was on my way to join him in the Seawards, when—"

"Yes, indeed. He will be wondering where you are."

"He certainly will."

"I imagine that his natural curiosity will bring him back in search of you. If not . . . well, we can consider what to do when the time comes." A little pause. "By the way, Mrs. Tibbett, how well do you know Miss Lucy?"

Once again, Emmy felt on firmer ground. "Hardly at all. We only met her when we drove over the other day to pay a courtesy call, as it were."

"But you've seen a lot of her since." It was a statement, not a question.

"Well . . ."

"I am just giving you a friendly warning, Mrs. Tibbett. She is a dangerous old woman and might seriously interfere with the deal we hope to make with your husband. In fact, I think it would be advisable if she went the way of the unlamented Brinkman. At her age, nobody would be surprised, and it would make the atmosphere altogether more congenial."

144

Carruthers stood up. "I'll leave you now. Annamabel will be outside your door. She will bring you your meals, and you can call her if you want to visit the bathroom. Meanwhile, all we can do is wait for Mr. Tibbett's return."

"Look here, Mr. Carruthers, you can't—"

It was too late. Using his own key, Carruthers had already opened the door and slipped out. Emmy heard the key turning again, and the voices of Carruthers and Annamabel outside in the passage. Emmy had no idea what they were saying. The too-good-to-be-true precise English had been replaced by rapid West Indian English, which is almost a patois and quite unintelligible to outsiders. Then the voices stopped, and Emmy heard Carruthers's quick, light footsteps retreating down the corridor. Exasperated and furious, she sat down on the bed and tried to think.

The first and most important thing was that Lucy was in danger and must be warned, protected, and somehow got off the island. The second, puzzling though it might be, was that Carruthers apparently believed Henry to be a drug dealer. If this was so, it must have been deliberately contrived by Henry, and Emmy cursed him for not telling her. Of course, he was not to know that she would be kidnapped—but she was appalled to think how nearly she had put her foot in things. The suggestion that De Marco and Brinkman were officers of the DEA she dismissed as pure fantasy. Carruthers evidently thought that Henry had had a hand in Brinkman's death. Had this idea, too, come from Henry himself?

Then, what about Sir Edward Ironmonger? Emmy trusted him implicitly—and yet, he had driven her to the airport and delivered her neatly into the hands of her abductors, while keeping well clear himself. Only Lucy was beyond suspicion—which brought her full circle.

Emmy decided that this mental merry-go-round was getting her nowhere, so she switched her concentration to the events of the previous evening. What could she remember? Being at Lucy's, of course, and Sir Edward arriving with the surprising news that Henry wanted her to join him in the Seawards. Ironmonger had been curiously grim and unfriendly. Why? Emmy had no idea, and he had not offered any explanation. He had simply told her to pack her bag quickly, as she was to catch the 7:15 plane. Emmy remembered that when she had returned to the drawing room with her suitcase, she had caught the words "Back to square one," spoken bitterly by Sir Edward. Emmy's entrance had caused an uneasy silence, and Lucy had appeared upset, even though she said good-bye with all her usual warmth.

The drive over the mountain to the airport had been silent and unhappy. Sir Edward had dropped her some distance from the airport entrance, bidden her a stiffly formal farewell, and driven off.

Inside the airport, Emmy remembered checking in at the desk, paying for her ticket, surrendering her suitcase, and seeing the clerk detach the Immigration form from her passport. And then . . . and then . . . her name. Somebody had called her name.

"Mrs. Tibbett?"

The soft voice broke Emmy's daydream. It was the voice she had heard at the airport.

There was a gentle tap at the door and the voice said again, "Mrs. Tibbett? May I come in?"

Emmy stood up. "Of course, Mrs. Carruthers. If you have a key."

There were whispers in the corridor. Then the key turned in the lock, the door opened a fraction, and Carmelita

Carruthers slipped into the room. Instantly, the door was locked behind her.

"How nice to see you," said Emmy dryly. "Perhaps you can explain this extraordinary situation."

Carmelita looked ill and haggard with worry. She said, "Oh, Mrs. Tibbett, I'm so sorry. I . . . I don't know what to say. . . ."

"You called to me at the airport." Emmy was wrinkling her brow, remembering. "You were sitting at the bar. I went over and you bought me a drink. That's the last thing I remember."

"I've said I'm sorry."

"That has nothing to do with it. I want to know—why?"

Carmelita ignored this. Urgently, she said, "Have you got it?"

"Got what?"

"Oh, Mrs. Tibbett—you promised!"

"Promised what?"

Carmelita looked down. "You know what."

Emmy said, "Cocaine?"

Carmelita nodded silently.

"How could I promise you what I don't have?"

"Your husband has it."

Emmy began to see a glimmer of light among the idiocies. "I'm afraid somebody tricked you, Mrs. Carruthers. My husband isn't even in Tampica."

Carmelita raised her tear-filled eyes to Emmy's. "The cocaine. You promised."

"I promised you nothing." Emmy was very firm. "But I daresay somebody did. When did you leave Dr. Duncan's clinic in St. Mark's?"

"How did you know about that?"

147

"Never mind how I know. When did you leave?"

"Yesterday."

Emmy remembered what Lucy had said. "You got a fix?"

"Yes."

"Where from?"

"I don't know."

"For God's sake." Emmy's impatience was showing. "You must know. Somebody gave you a fix in St. Mark's, and you left the clinic and came back here. Somebody told you that either Henry or I would provide the next installment. Who was that person?"

Embarrassingly, the lovely black woman began to weep uncontrollably. "Stop asking questions. Give me. Give me the white girl."

"The white—" Emmy began, and then remembered the West Indian street name for cocaine. "I've told you I can't give you what I don't have. Now—who gave it to you in St. Mark's?"

Carmelita sniffed. "I swear I don't know. I was in Doc Duncan's place. A nurse brought me a box of chocolates. From a friend, she said. Inside, under the chocolates . . . oh, it was so good. I felt strong and wonderful. It was easy to get out. Doc never locks the doors."

"Doc Duncan," said Emmy, who knew that venerable, wicked, saintly old man, "would never hold anyone against their will. You don't want to be cured, do you?"

"Of course not."

"All right, get on with it. You took a plane to Tampica. Who told you that Henry and I had drugs to sell?"

The exquisite black eyebrows went up. "To sell? You think I buy the white girl? Me—Carmelita? You *give* me—you hear, you *give* me."

"Oh, don't be silly."

"It is you who are silly." Carmelita had stopped weeping and sounded sly. "You need favor from Chester, yes? So you give me what I want."

"You didn't know that Henry had left Tampica, did you?" Emmy changed the subject firmly.

"Is not important. You give me."

"Perhaps I will, " said Emmy slowly, "if you get me out of here."

"I don't understand."

"Of course you do. Somebody—with your help—kidnapped me at the airport and brought me here. You know very well I'm being held as a prisoner, or perhaps a hostage. I want to know why, and I want to get away."

"Chester's not so bad guy," said Carmelita thoughtfully. "Only silly."

"What's that supposed to mean?"

"So silly—he don't even know I love the white girl. I t'ink he beat me bad if he know." Carmelita had dropped into her natural West Indian manner of speech. "You give me good fix, I make everyt'ing right with Chester." She looked greedily at Emmy. "Where is?"

"You don't expect me to—?"

"Suitcase. Where is suitcase?"

At that moment the key turned in the lock, and Annamabel's head came round the door, her eyes rolling.

"He comin'! He comin'!"

Carmelita was out of the door like a black shadow. Emmy heard a car drawing up outside her shuttered window. A door opened and slammed shut. There were masculine voices and footsteps.

"You need not have driven round here, sir. My man would

149

have parked the car for you." Chester Carruthers sounded very slightly rattled.

"No trouble, Mr. Carruthers. I'll leave her here with the key in, shall I?" It was Henry's voice.

Emmy ran to the window and began to beat on the wooden shutters. No good, of course. The footsteps and voices grew faint as the two men rounded the corner of the house. All the same, Emmy's heart soared. Henry would never have come up to The Lodge unless he had a shrewd suspicion that she was here.

Quickly, she went to the wardrobe, took out her case, and opened it. As she had thought, it was undisturbed. Or was it? Gingerly, she started turning over the neatly folded skirts, shirts, and underwear. At the bottom were the high-heeled court shoes that she had worn for the flight from England, and had since forgotten about. She slipped her hand inside one of them. The toe was crammed with small plastic envelopes, and she was not in the least surprised to find that they contained an innocent-looking white powder, much like bicarbonate of soda: the white girl.

12

enry sat on the wide veranda of The Lodge, a glass of rum punch in his hand, looking out over the neatly tended gardens down to Tampica Harbour and the sea beyond. Opposite him, Chester Carruthers smiled merrily and raised his glass.

"Welcome back to Tampica, Mr. Tibbett. We were beginning to think we had seen the last of you. You prefer the British Seawards to our little island?"

"I wouldn't say that, Mr. Prime Minister. I have grown very attached to Tampica during this holiday." Henry tipped his glass toward Carruthers and drank. "As a matter of fact, though, I had intended to spend a few more days on St. Mark's—with my wife."

A pause. Politely, Carruthers said, "Oh, yes? But you changed your mind."

"It was changed for me." Henry matched smile for smile. "You see, my wife never reached the Seawards. She has disappeared."

"Disappeared? That sounds very dramatic."

"It's very worrying," said Henry. "So I have come to ask you for your help in finding her."

"I don't see what help I could give you."

"I believe you know where she is, Mr. Carruthers."

"Well, now, Mr. Tibbett, I would not exactly say that. But I admit that I have heard rumors. I think it likely that she is somewhere on Tampica."

"That's what I think, too." Henry kept his voice level and pleasant. "I also think that her freedom of movement has been curtailed, and I ask myself why."

Carruthers leaned back in his chair. "It could be, Mr. Tibbett, that she has been used to lure you back to us. I think there are some people anxious to talk business with you."

"It seems a curious way of doing business, Mr. Prime Minister."

Carruthers's smile widened. "This is the Caribbean, Mr. Tibbett. We tend to do things differently."

"So I see."

"In England or the United States she would be in prison. Here we are more relaxed. I like to think more humane also."

"I don't understand you."

"Oh, come now, Mr. Tibbett. You are pulling my leg."

Henry said nothing. Carruthers went on, "You can't ask me to believe that you did not know that your wife was carrying a considerable quantity of cocaine in her suitcase when she attempted to leave Tampica. However, our police force is very efficient. She was apprehended at the airport."

Henry said, "That's not what Commissioner Kelly told the British Consul in Barbados. He swore that she was not and never had been in custody, and that she had left Tampica."

Carruthers waved an airy hand. "My dear Tibbett, Kelly was simply protecting your wife's good name. The act of a perfect gentleman, I should have thought. Surely you would not have wished the consul to be told the truth?"

"I see." Henry took a sip of rum punch. "So what are your terms?"

"I beg your pardon, Mr. Tibbett?"

"You say you wish to do business with me. What sort of business?"

"I think you know, Mr. Tibbett. We understand that you are interested in making a substantial investment in this island. Round about two million United States dollars. That is so, is it not?"

Henry considered. "If I should make this investment, what would I get in return—apart from my wife's freedom?"

"We could offer you—certain facilities. More than that I cannot say for the moment." With an abrupt change of tone, he added sharply, "What do you know of Brinkman's death?"

"Only that it was not accidental."

"You know that he and De Marco were both agents of the Drug Enforcement Agency?"

"I know now."

"They were trying to trap some of our more gullible citizens into buying dangerous drugs. Fortunately we—that is to say, the Tampican authorities—realized their game in time. Brinkman, as you know, is dead. De Marco—whatever his real name may be—will not be allowed to enter Tampica again. The United States has no right to act as *agent provocateur* in another sovereign country." Carruthers was putting on a fine act of moral indignation.

Henry said, mildly, "Do you really think that was what they were trying to do?"

Again, the smile. "What else, Mr. Tibbett?"

Reflectively, Henry said, "Two million dollars is a lot of money, Mr. Carruthers. If I were to invest that amount in Tampica, I would expect considerable cooperation when it came to my import-export business."

"Indeed? I understood from Ironmonger that you had retired."

"Not completely. I still have certain interests. I do some

153

shipping of cargo from South America to the United States. Tampica is very conveniently situated between the two."

Carruthers stood up. "I don't think these are matters which we can discuss here and now."

Henry, too, got to his feet. He said, "We can't discuss anything, least of all my possible investments, until my wife is free and all charges against her dropped."

"That may take a little time, Mr. Tibbett."

"Then you had better get moving, Mr. Carruthers. My time is not unlimited, and there are other islands in which I could invest." Henry looked straight at Carruthers. "Where is my wife, Mr. Prime Minister?"

"I'm sorry, Mr. Tibbett. I really do not know exactly. I shall have to consult with Police Commissioner Kelly."

"She is not in this house, by any chance?"

"My dear Tibbett, I—"

It was at this moment that the louvered doors from the drawing room opened and Emmy stepped out onto the terrace.

"Hello, darling," she said to Henry, "I thought I heard your voice." She smiled. "Good morning again, Mr. Carruthers."

Chester Carruthers looked as if he would explode. "Mrs. Tibbett! What on earth are you doing here?"

Evenly, Emmy said, "I have enjoyed your hospitality, Mr. Carruthers, but I think the time has come to leave. Henry and I will be going back to the Seawards on the next plane, and I hope this time nobody will try to stop us."

Carruthers had pulled himself together. He said, "Just a moment, Mrs. Tibbett. I am afraid you are not free to leave Tampica. There is a charge of possession of a controlled substance—"

"Is there?" Emmy smiled again. "It's the first I have heard of it."

Grimly, Carruthers said, "I must ask you both to sit down while I make a phone call." He picked up the telephone from the terrace table. "Ask Commissioner Kelly to come here at once. And tell the guards that nobody is to leave this compound without my personal authorization." He put down the telephone and resumed his smile. "Let me order drinks for you both. I wouldn't advise you to try to leave. The gate is guarded, as you know, and the grounds patrolled by Dobermans. However, if you stay just here, you will be quite safe, and we can get this matter sorted out."

Emmy glanced a question at Henry, who nodded. Carruthers shouted for a servant and ordered three rum punches. When the drinks had been served, Emmy said, "Aren't you going to ask me how I got out of that locked room, Mr. Carruthers?"

"Locked room, Mrs. Tibbett? I fear you have been suffering from delusions. You won't deny that when you arrived here last night you were under the influence of drugs?"

"I was under the influence of something that was administered to me without my knowledge." Emmy was finding it hard to remain calm. "So you mean to say I have had the freedom of your house ever since—"

"Ever since you were arrested for being in possession of dangerous drugs, Mrs. Tibbett."

Henry said, "That two-million-dollar investment is beginning to look less and less attractive, Mr. Carruthers."

"All the same, I think you will find it a good bargain," said Carruthers smoothly. "However, while we wait for Commissioner Kelly, let us talk of other things. Like Mr. Brinkman's accident, for instance."

"I've already told Kelly that it wasn't an accident," said Henry.

"So you have, Mr. Tibbett. Strange that you should admit it so readily. Commissioner Kelly was telling me only yesterday that he hopes to make an arrest very soon. He feels that there was only one person with both motive and opportunity for the crime—if there was a crime. I admit that extradition proceedings from the British Seawards might have taken a little time, but now that you have come back here voluntarily—well, let us hope that it does not come to that. We still have the death penalty in this country, you know."

Henry sat back in his chair. "You have the strangest way of doing business, Mr. Carruthers. I can't help feeling that I am not the right sort of investor for Tampica." He hoped that he had the phrase right.

"Oh, but I think you are, Mr. Tibbett. It's just a question of give and take—you do us a favor, we return it, everybody is happy, and all deals are profitable."

"The only favor you can do me," said Henry, "is to facilitate the transit of my goods through Tampica, as I explained earlier." Emmy's eyebrows rose a fraction, but she said nothing. "Your threats of arresting my wife for drug possession and myself for murder are simply pathetic."

"You think so? I rather doubt—ah, this must be Kelly now."

One of the familiar black government cars was nosing around a bend in the graveled driveway, and as it pulled to a halt below the terrace, the lanky Police Commissioner climbed out of the backseat. He said something to the chauffeur, who at once drove the car on around the corner of the house. Kelly ran up the steps to the veranda.

"You wanted to see me, Chester? I've just—" He stopped abruptly as he saw Henry and Emmy.

"I think you know Mr. and Mrs. Tibbett, Desmond." Carruthers might have been hosting a diplomatic cocktail party. "We were just discussing investment possibilities. Meanwhile, they seem anxious to be off to the Seawards. Do you have any objections to their leaving Tampica?"

Kelly opened his mouth and then shut it again. The look of appeal that he shot at Carruthers was desperate. Clearly, he had not been briefed.

Carruthers smiled sympathetically and went on, "I understand there was some problem about certain objects found by our customs officer in Mrs. Tibbett's suitcase."

"Ah, yes." Relief flooded Kelly's face. "The suitcase. Yes. Quite. Very much so. The suitcase contained cocaine."

"Did you confiscate it?" It was obvious that Carruthers knew the answer to this question, because he went straight on. "No, no, of course not. You did not want to embarrass a distinguished guest with a formal arrest and remand in prison. I suggest that we might examine the suitcase now."

"My suitcase!" Emmy exclaimed. "There's nothing in my suitcase except my clothes!"

"We shall see." Carruthers pressed a bell, and a white-coated servant appeared. "Ah, Manuel. Please ask Annamabel to bring Mrs. Tibbett's suitcase out here."

Henry felt a sudden surge of fear. Of course, cocaine would have been planted in Emmy's suitcase. He looked at her untroubled face and longed to be able to warn her, to be able to . . . The louvered doors opened again, and coal-black Annamabel waddled onto the terrace. She put Emmy's suitcase on the table, and went in again without a word.

Carruthers said, "Please search the suitcase, Desmond.

And Mrs. Tibbett, please watch him carefully. I would not like you to think there had been any hanky-panky."

Very deliberately, Kelly began taking everything out of the case. Skirts, shirts, underwear, sponge-bag, hairbrush, cosmetics, talcum powder, and finally shoes, the insides of which he inspected carefully. In a few moments, the case was empty. Kelly looked up in angry amazement.

"There's nothing there!" he shouted. "She must have got rid of it!"

"Impossible." Carruthers was on his feet. "Have her room searched! There was no way she could have—" He stopped.

Emmy said, "No way I could have got out, Mr. Carruthers? Quite right. As you well know, I was locked in. By all means search the room."

"I'll do it myself!" Kelly almost ran into the house. Henry looked at Emmy, and she gave him an almost imperceptible wink. Relief surged through him. He had, as usual, underestimated her. How had she done it? Well, he would find out in good time. Meanwhile, Kelly reappeared, angrier than ever. He had found nothing. Annamabel, he added, admitted letting Mrs. Tibbett out and escorting her down to the terrace. There was no way she could have disposed of anything *en route*.

Henry stood up. "Well," he said, "I think that disposes of the case against my wife. We will be leaving now."

Furiously, Carruthers said, "Not so fast, Mr. Tibbett. There is the matter of Mr. Brinkman's death." He turned to Kelly. "Well?"

The Police Commissioner hesitated. "No charges have yet been—"

Henry said, "You will now stop this nonsense. It so

happens that I have a witness who saw the murderer and can describe him."

"I am sure you have, Mr. Tibbett. How much did you pay your witness?"

"This conversation," said Henry, "is absolutely ludicrous. Nobody would imagine that we were about to enter into an important business deal. Come along, Emmy. If the deal still interests you, Mr. Carruthers, you can find me at the Anchorage Inn on St. Matthew's." He picked up Emmy's suitcase, took her arm, and led her down the steps. At the bottom, he turned and said, "Please countermand your orders to the guards at the gate. We shall be driving out in a couple of minutes."

A little over two minutes later, Henry drove his hired car through the gates of The Lodge and down the hill, headed for Tampica Harbour and the airport. Nobody attempted to stop him.

In the car, Emmy began, "Henry, what on earth—?"

Henry said, "Let's just concentrate on getting out of here. Explanations later."

So the car was handed over to Barney's representative at the airport, tickets were bought and check-ins completed, and Henry and Emmy just had time for a much-needed sandwich before the British Seaward Airways flight to St. Mark's was announced. Ilicia Murphy was at the desk and looked curiously at the Tibbetts—but clearly she had had no instructions, and they boarded the plane with a handful of other passengers. In the air, engine noise made conversation impossible. So it was not until the Tibbetts were in St. Mark's, sitting in the drawing room at Government House with Sir Alfred Pendleton, that the situation could be sorted out.

"First of all, Sir Alfred," Emmy said, "we have to warn Lucy."

"Warn her?"

"Carruthers suspects, of all things, that Lucy is suspicious of Henry and me. He talked about her having an accident, like Brinkman. Can you call her? I don't think I should."

"No, of course not, Mrs. Tibbett. I'll do it from my study."

"Tell her I'm here and safe," Emmy said. "And tell her not to trust anybody. Not anybody. And to get away from Tampica."

"Will do, Mrs. Tibbett."

A few minutes later, Pendleton was back, chuckling to himself. "Well, I told her," he said. "She's delighted that you're here, but as for running away herself—well, you can imagine her reaction. Now, Tibbett, let's hear what happened."

When Henry had finished his story, Emmy looked at him in amazement. "Drug Enforcement agents? Are you absolutely sure, Henry?"

"Of course I'm sure. Sir Alfred will bear me out."

The Governor nodded.

"Now you're supposed to be taking over where they left off?"

"That's the general idea. And now—what happened to you?"

"I don't remember much of it, at least the beginning part," Emmy admitted. "I checked in for my flight and the girl had just weighed and tagged my suitcase, when I heard my name called. There was a group of people having a drink at the bar, and they asked me to join them."

"Who was in this group?"

"The only one I can remember was Carmelita Carruthers.

160

It was she who called me over. Somebody gave me a drink—and after that everything is a blank, until I woke up in what must have been a maid's room at The Lodge. Locked in, of course, and guarded by that large black lady who brought down my suitcase. Carruthers himself came in after breakfast and talked. I couldn't make out what on earth he was driving at—but of course I understand now. He knew about De Marco and Brinkman—that is, Wright and Stevenson—and he thought you were a drug dealer. Thank goodness I don't think I said anything indiscreet. Then, after he'd gone, Carmelita arrived."

"What on earth did she want?" Henry asked.

Emmy made a face. "Cocaine. What she called the white girl. Chester doesn't know it, or so she says, but she's an addict. Actually, I knew already, from Lucy. She was supposed to be at Dr. Duncan's clinic here, taking the cure, but somebody slipped her a fix in a box of candy, and she ran away from the clinic and went back to Tampica yesterday. Somebody also told her that she could get the stuff from me. She said that if I'd give it to her, she'd get me out. Naturally, I said I couldn't, because I didn't have any. She obviously didn't believe me. After she'd gone, two things happened. I heard you arrive, and I found a whole lot of cocaine in my suitcase."

"So what did you do?"

Emmy grinned. "What do you think? I got Annamabel to call Carmelita back, and struck the deal. She got the cocaine, and I got out of my prison."

"Emmy, you shouldn't have—"

"She'd have got it from somewhere," Emmy said. "I had to get out of there, and I had to get rid of the beastly stuff."

Sir Alfred began to laugh. "Very neat, my dear," he said. "Very neat. So here you both are, and what happens next?"

"Next," said Henry, "we take the ferry over to St. Matthew's and stay at the Anchorage Inn."

"You know your friends the Colvilles have left and gone back to England? We all miss them." Sir Alfred lit his pipe. "Still, I believe the inn is still very charming, under the new management. But what about your mission?"

Henry said, "I've already told Carruthers that he'd have to come to St. Matthew's if he wanted to talk business with me. It was the only way I could think of to lure him into British jurisdiction. I don't have a boat, as Wright did, and anyhow he's obviously suspicious of that ploy by now. The fact that he threatened to frame Emmy for drug possession and me for murder, to twist my arm, means that he's desperate for money. It also played into my hands, making it quite natural that I should refuse to stay on Tampica. I think he'll come."

"I'll alert the St. Matthew's police and send a couple of extra officers over there," the Governor promised. "If Carruthers or anyone else from Tampica contacts you, let me know at once. We'll set up the meeting so that they won't have a chance of getting away with it. Good luck, Tibbett."

So Henry and Emmy took the ferry to the island of St. Matthew's, which held many memories for them, and took a room at the small, white-painted inn that had been their home base for other adventures. They regretted the absence of John and Margaret Colville, but soon struck up a pleasant relationship with the new owners—a burly islander called Jim and his slender, paler-skinned wife, Janette.

There was nothing to do but wait, and speculate. Meanwhile, they revisited old haunts—swimming from creamy white beaches and walking through the rain forest of the island's central peak, among wild white orchids and sweet-smelling frangipani. They did not venture into the august precincts of the St. Matthew's Golf Club, reputed to be the most exclusive and expensive resort in the world. From the outside, it still resembled a top-security prison, and they wondered idly what superstars of stage, screen, and politics were basking in luxury behind the barricades.

On their second day, looking down on the little harbor of Priest Town from a clearing in the mountainside, they were not altogether surprised to see the dark blue hull of *Bellissima* nosing through the channel in the encircling reef.

"Poor Agent Wright," said Emmy. "His mission ended in tragedy and failure, but I can understand that he still wants to be in at the kill."

"As a matter of fact," Henry said, "Wright told me that he was bringing *Bellissima* back here, as it's her home port. He plans to send young Porter home, and I suppose he'll go back to the States himself. All the same, I wish he hadn't turned up just now. It might be awkward, and Sir Alfred must have told him about our plans to get the Tampicans here. I just hope he clears off as fast as possible."

"Well, I find it's rather comforting to know he's here." Emmy paused, and then added, "It seems a shame, after all his work, that if you do pull this off, the culprits will be arrested by the British and not by the Americans."

"I don't think that'll worry him," Henry assured her. "All that the DEA wants is to see Carruthers and his lot behind bars."

On the third day, just before lunchtime, Henry was told that there was a telephone call for him.

"Tibbett speaking."

"Mr. Tibbett. What a pleasure. This is Joe Palmer from Tampica."

"What can I do for you, Mr. Palmer?"

"The Prime Minister is very anxious that you and Mrs. Tibbett should come back to Tampica to discuss your possible investment, sir."

"I'm sure he is," said Henry. "However, as I made clear to him, if he wants to talk to me, he comes here. We have no intention of visiting Tampica again. As you may have heard, he didn't exactly play his cards very tactfully last week."

Palmer hesitated, then said, "It's a matter of your credentials, Mr. Tibbett. After all, you know all about us, but we know very little about you. There are two sides to every bargain, you know."

"Naturally. We can talk about all these things when we meet. As to credentials, I have always been a great believer in the maxim that money talks."

"What sort of money are we discussing, Mr. Tibbett?"

"Why don't you come over and find out?" said Henry, pleasantly. "Good-bye, Mr. Palmer."

He hung up, and immediately lifted the receiver again and dialed the number of Government House in St. Mark's.

"Sir Alfred? Tibbett here. Sorry to bother you, but I need half a million dollars in cash. In a hurry."

"Good God, man. What for?"

"Bait."

"You've had a nibble, then?"

"I have."

"How and when do you need this money?"

"Within the next two days. In used notes, not too high denominations."

Sir Alfred sighed. "Today is Sunday. I'll get moving on it tomorrow and do what I can."

Exactly what Sir Alfred did do, Henry never knew, although it must have involved both Washington and London.

In any case, on Monday afternoon he was again called to the telephone.

"Tibbett? Pendleton. I shall have it tomorrow morning. You'll have to come and get it."

"Not me," said Henry promptly. "I have to stay here. I'll send Emmy."

"I think she should have a police escort."

"Good Lord, no. Just a biggish handbag, or—yes, that's it. Emmy will go to St. Mark's to do some shopping. Can you get hold of suitable plastic shopping bags from local stores?"

"I thought perhaps a suitcase—"

"No. Plastic shopping bags."

"Very well, Tibbett."

"She'll be on the early ferry," said Henry. "Thank you very much, sir."

"My pleasure." Pendleton chuckled. "Good luck."

Emmy was none too pleased when Henry told her about her assignment, but she took Henry's point that they were possibly being watched, and that any such expedition on his part would arouse suspicion. So at eight the next morning she boarded the interisland ferry, having let it be known at the Anchorage Inn that she intended to have a shopping spree on St. Mark's. And Henry settled down in the open-air bar of the inn to do a crossword puzzle and wait for a telephone call.

It came at midday—from a soft-spoken West Indian secretary. The Prime Minister of Tampica, she said, had asked her to call Mr. Tibbett. He and Mrs. Carruthers, together with Mr. and Mrs. Palmer, were planning to visit St. Matthew's the following day, Wednesday. They would be pleased if Mr. and Mrs. Tibbett would join them for luncheon at the Anchorage Inn. One o'clock? Thank you very much, Mr. Tibbett.

13

Emmy came back to St. Matthew's on the afternoon ferry, carrying two bulging plastic shopping bags bearing the names of St. Mark's two biggest stores. At the Anchorage, she dropped them onto the bed with a great sigh of relief.

"Whew! I'm glad that's over. I had no idea money could weigh so much!"

Henry grinned at her. "Well, it worked. They're coming for lunch tomorrow. The Carruthers and the Palmers."

"So—what's the form?"

"I've alerted the Governor and the Police Commissioner," Henry told her, "and the dining room is wired for sound. We've just been testing it. Jim and Janette have agreed to let us have it to ourselves."

"Police?" Emmy queried.

"They'll be listening in, but I daren't risk having any of them hanging around. At a prearranged moment—when I give them a code phrase on the recorder—they'll close in. That'll be when we have enough evidence to make the arrests. We've got to be careful, because these people will certainly be armed— and look what happened to poor Agent Stevenson."

"You think they did it?"

"I think it's very likely. They found out that Wright and Stevenson were DEA men. Stevenson was the easy one to get, because of his parasailing. They made a halfhearted attempt to make it look like an accident, but Wright got the message at once."

"I see." Emmy ran a hand through her curly black hair, and sat down on the bed. "I hope I'm not supposed to take part in any of this. I'd be quite useless, and I never want to see either of the Carrutherses again."

"You must lunch with us." Henry was quite definite. "Naturally they think we're in this together, and it would be suspicious if you didn't show up. However, after coffee you should suggest showing the ladies round the gardens. That'll just seem normal and tactful—leaving the men to get on with business. I don't suppose they want their wives mixed up in it, anyway."

"I don't much like the idea of leaving you alone with those two." Emmy was dubious.

"Don't worry." Henry patted the bulging shopping bags. "I shall have the most potent persuader right there with me."

"I hope you're right."

"And now, there's a telephone call I want you to make. Listen carefully and remember exactly what I say . . ."

About an hour after this conversation took place at the Anchorage Inn, a very different one was taking place at Sugar Mill House on Tampica. Sir Edward Ironmonger was talking to Lucy Pontefract-Deacon, and he was very angry.

"A complete washout." He sipped his drink furiously. "I must say, Lucy, I see now it was an extremely foolish idea of yours to get Tibbett over here. He has done far worse than nothing—he has simply alerted De Marco and Carruthers that something is up. And now he and his imbecile wife have skipped off to the Seawards, leaving us to cope."

Lucy raised her eyebrows. "Mrs. Tibbett is in the Seawards?"

"You know very well she is. I drove her to the airport myself."

Lucy gave the Governor-General a long look over the rim of her glass, which she was holding in both hands. Then she said, "I agree with you, Eddie. I'm sure Henry did his best, but we're none of us getting any younger, and this was a tricky assignment. So what are you and I going to do, eh?"

"What can we do?" Sir Edward was irritable. "For the moment, nothing. Tibbett imagines that De Marco will carry on where he left off, but I don't. For a start, *Bellissima* has left Tampica."

"She has?" Lucy was interested. "Where's she bound?"

"She got Customs clearance from here to Antigua, but she may well have moved on from there by now. All I know is, she's not back here. If you ask me, her mission is aborted, and we'll have to wait until they try again."

"Perhaps we will," said Lucy, slowly and thoughtfully. Her musings were cut short by a brisk rapping on the front door. "Excuse me, Eddie. Samuel has gone home already, so I must go and answer it."

Ironmonger stood up. "I'm off anyway," he said. "We'll keep in touch."

"We'll do that, Eddie," said Miss Pontefract-Deacon. There was another, more forceful knock on the door. "All right, all right!" She added, for her unseen visitor, "I'm coming!"

But when Lucy opened the front door, there was nobody there: only a small envelope lying on the raffia mat in the hall. Instinctively, she put her size eight blue sneaker over it, as Ironmonger followed her out of the drawing room.

"Who was it?" he asked.

"Nobody, Eddie. Just some children playing the fool. Goodbye, dear."

Lucy waited until the big black car was out of the driveway before she removed her foot and picked up the envelope.

Chester Carruthers and Joseph Palmer, complete with Carmelita and Emmalinda, arrived on the ferry from St. Mark's at noon the next day, having taken the early plane from Tampica. Henry and Emmy were at the quayside to meet them, with a long-bodied, six-seater hired Jeep to drive the party to the Anchorage Inn.

"Not quite what you're accustomed to in the way of transport, I'm afraid," said Henry, as he helped Emmalinda Palmer heave her considerable bulk up into the back of the vehicle. She responded with her usual merry peal of laughter.

"No problem, Mr. Tibbett. No problem." She settled herself into a space intended for at least two people, arranging her flowing purple caftan about her knees. It was fortunate that Carmelita, who seemed in high spirits, occupied only half a place on the bench seat. Carruthers and Palmer climbed into the back seat, facing their wives, Emmy jumped into the front seat beside Henry, and the Jeep roared away from the jetty and up the hill to the Anchorage Inn.

Once there, Chester Carruthers looked critically around the empty bar, open to the breezes, with its palm-frond roof and simple furniture. With his unwavering smile firmly in place, he said, "I find it a little unusual, Mr. Tibbett, that you should not be staying at the Golf Club."

"You surprise me, Mr. Prime Minister," said Henry. "The Golf Club is altogether too conspicuous a place for conducting private business."

"It has a great reputation for privacy and discretion," Carruthers pointed out.

"Privacy from outsiders," Henry agreed. He left the rest of the remark unsaid.

Carruthers's smile deepened. "I see what you mean."

Janette, the landlady, appeared behind the bar, served drinks, and withdrew. Joe Palmer joined Henry and Carruthers, leaving the three women alone at the far end of the bar.

"A charming spot, the British Seawards," he remarked, in his careful English. "But I wonder why these islands have not followed us into independence."

"In some respects," said Henry, "I think they may be more independent than you are."

The two black men looked at him with undisguised hostility. Then Carruthers replaced his usually unfailing smile. "I wonder what you mean by that, Mr. Tibbett?"

Equally smiling, Henry said, "They have complete internal autonomy, as you well know, and they also have the power of Great Britain behind them on matters of defense. This makes them very independent, I would say."

Palmer gave a short and unamused laugh. "Except from the United Kingdom."

"The United Kingdom is an undemanding master," said Henry, lightly.

"Tampica has no masters," said Palmer angrily.

"No?" Henry drained his glass. "I am very glad to hear it. Will you have another drink, gentlemen, or shall we go in to lunch?"

As promised, the dining room, which led off the bar, was empty of other diners. A table for six had been attractively set, with a pink cotton tablecloth and deeper pink treble hibiscus flowers laid by each plate and piled into a centerpiece. Only Henry knew that the flowers concealed a tiny voice-activated recorder, and that the small microphones connecting the room to the police listening post were hidden

170

in the woven basketwork lampshade, in the shape of a deep bowl, which hung above the table.

The lunch, served by Janette, was delicious. Crisply delicate conch fritters—the pieces of shellfish in creamy sauce dipped in bread crumbs and deep-fried—were followed by a dish of chicken and rice, spicy with hot peppers and fresh ginger in the West Indian manner. As a fitting conclusion, Janette came out from the kitchen with a blazing dish of bananas baked in sugar, butter, and lime juice and flambéed in rum.

"You wouldn't get a meal like this at the Golf Club," Henry remarked. And his guests wiped their mouths appreciatively on their pink cotton napkins and agreed with him.

Conversation over lunch had been deliberately general and noncontroversial. Emmalinda Palmer had eaten a lot, laughed a lot, and raised everybody's spirits. Carmelita played the sophisticated, witty politician's wife. Emmy could hardly believe that only a few days ago these people had held her prisoner, and Carmelita had been in tears pleading for a fix of the white girl. Much as she loved the Caribbean, Emmy found the role playing, the endless identity games, more than she could happily stand. She found herself longing for her own people—not all pleasant, perhaps, but on the whole predictable.

After coffee had been served, Emmy stood up and said, "I expect you ladies would like to freshen up in our bathroom. And then I can show you the gardens."

Carruthers gave an almost imperceptible nod to his wife, who stood up gracefully, saying, "How very kind, Mrs. Tibbett. I daresay the men have business to discuss."

Emalinda gave her robust, rumbling laugh. "Bizness, is it? Bad stories and dirty gossip, mo' like. De man an' dem is all same." But she lumbered to her feet and followed Emmy and

Carmelita out of the dining room and up the outside staircase to the Tibbetts' bedroom.

Henry said, "Well, gentlemen, shall we get down to brass tacks?" He looked at the other two. "What is your proposition? You can speak freely here."

Palmer and Carruthers exchanged a look. Then Carruthers said, "I think it is up to you to put the proposition, Mr. Tibbett."

Henry leaned back in his chair and wished he had not given up smoking. His pipe would have been a great comfort at that moment. He said, "I am empowered to offer you gentlemen two million United States dollars in cash in return for certain facilities on Tampica. As a mark of good faith, I have half a million right here, which I will hand to you as soon as a satisfactory bargain has been struck."

"What facilities?" demanded Palmer.

Henry raised his eyebrows. "Surely there is no need to ask that, Mr. Palmer?"

"I think we may take it," Carruthers put in smoothly, "that Mr. Tibbett wishes unimpeded entry into and exit from Tampica for certain cargoes from South America, en route to the United States."

"For how long a period?" Palmer, to Henry's envy, lit up a cigar. "Two million is not very much, by today's standards. I would suggest six months."

"A year," said Henry flatly. "The arrangement to be renegotiated in one year's time."

"A year is too long." Carruthers was very definite. "Let us compromise on eight months."

"Nine," said Henry. They glared at each other. Then Carruthers smiled his unfailing smile. "Very well. We will accommodate you, Mr. Tibbett. Nine months. Now—how will the cargo arrive?"

172

"Some by boat, some by light plane." Henry sounded brisk and businesslike. "One or other of you gentlemen will be notified of details in advance, by a code which I will explain later. It will be up to you to ensure that the cargoes are not examined by anybody, official or otherwise, and that they are safely stored until onward transmission is arranged. Once again, you will be informed in code. We plan to use quite a number of small private boats—pleasure yachts—as well as aircraft for onward transmission."

"To Florida?" Palmer asked.

Henry smiled. "That is entirely our affair. Once the cargo leaves Tampica—"

He broke off as Emmy and her two companions walked past the window and into the garden. Palmer glanced briefly at the women, and then said, "Naturally, our wives know nothing about these . . . em . . . business arrangements which we occasionally make. I take it that your wife is not in the same position?"

"She is aware of the nature of my profession," said Henry. "Now, there is one question I must ask you before committing myself in any way."

"Ask on, my dear fellow." Carruthers waved a hand, airily. "Ask on."

"Before the unfortunate episode of De Marco and Brinkman—by the way, I must congratulate you on your handling of that—I presume you had an arrangement similar to the one we are now discussing. What went wrong with it?"

There was a silence. Palmer studied the glowing tip of his cigar, and then glanced at Carruthers. Carruthers said briefly, "The people concerned could not meet our price."

Henry's eyebrows went up. "*Could* not? Surely you mean *would* not?"

173

Palmer waved his cigar airily. "Could or would makes little difference. Let us say they *did* not."

"I can't believe," said Henry, "that you would deal with anybody who could not afford a mere two million. It occurs to me that perhaps the facilities you provided were unsatisfactory."

"How dare you suggest that?" Joe Palmer was very angry. "We kept precisely to our side of the bargain."

"And what exactly did the cargo consist of?"

Again, an exchanged glance. Henry held his breath. It was vital to get these men to name the drugs, otherwise a clever lawyer could run circles around the police in court.

At last, Carruthers said, "You have not specified the nature of your cargo, Mr. Tibbett."

"No, I haven't, have I?" Henry smiled. "I think we are all—what shall I say—inhibited over that. We don't entirely trust each other, and in my case—after what happened to my wife—I think you will agree that I am justified." A pause. "However, if you insist, I will specify. There will be a certain amount of bulky cargo, by which I mean, of course, marijuana. I imagine you will want to keep quite a lot of it in Tampica, as I understand it is the substance most favored and most traditional to your people."

Carruthers nodded slowly, but did not speak. "However," Henry went on, "the valuable and of course more lightweight consignments will be high-grade pure cocaine."

Carruthers said, "How will it arrive? By sea or air?"

"That depends." Henry was careful to conceal his relief. He had named the drugs and Carruthers had made no protest. "You will be notified, as I said." He paused. "By the way, I notice that Commissioner Kelly is not with you. I hope there will be no trouble from that quarter."

174

Carruthers said, "I congratulate you on your perception, Mr. Tibbett. Always in the past Kelly has been completely with us. However, recently he seems to be—how shall I put it—holding back a little."

"So what do you intend to do about it?" Henry asked sharply.

Carruthers smiled. "There is always the possibility that he might have an accident," he said. "Like poor Mr. Brinkman."

"That would be very unwise," said Henry. "Surely you can think of a better alternative?"

"What do you suggest?" This from Palmer.

Henry said, "As a start, I would send him to another island—as far away as possible—on a training course for senior executives. Even possibly to the U.S. mainland. If there is to be an accident, it should not be on Tampica."

Carruthers nodded. "Yes, that is an ingenious idea. With your help—"

"Mine?" Henry sounded surprised.

"Come, come, Mr. Tibbett. You and your friends can arrange such things."

"Possibly," said Henry dryly. "Meanwhile, who is to be Police Commissioner? He must obviously be reliable."

"No need to worry there," said Palmer. "Kelly's immediate deputy has been . . . on our payroll, as you might say . . . for some time. He will take over temporarily and finally be confirmed in the post. I see no difficulty."

"During my stay in Tampica," Henry said, "I had time to observe some of your more prominent characters. It occurs to me that Ironmonger could be a problem."

"Ironmonger is a fool." Chester Carruthers sounded faintly amused. "Oh, an upright, law-abiding fool, but a fool nevertheless. We can easily take care of him at any time. He is also vulnerable, because he has a mistress. Everyone on Tampica knows about it, but it would embarrass him greatly if it was broadcast outside the island. Meanwhile, it is useful to us to have a man of his impeccable reputation as Governor-General."

"Yes. Yes, I can see that." Henry sounded thoughtful. "Then there's the old woman. I went to see her, of course."

"We are well aware of that." Palmer blew aromatic smoke over the table.

"You tried to persuade me that she was senile," Henry went on. "My impression is that she is very much all there. She might be dangerous."

"Dangerous?" Carruthers laughed. "My dear Tibbett, she's almost ninety. I admit that she was influential in the old days, but there's nothing she can do now."

"She could tell—"

"Tell whom? The British? They have no power to meddle in the affairs of a sovereign state. In any case, where would she get her proof? If you really think it advisable, nothing would be easier than to dispose of her, but I really think you are conjuring up jumbies."

Henry looked at him, a hard stare. "Talking of jumbies, Mr. Carruthers, do you know that Dolphin saw one, on the morning of Brinkman's death?"

"Dolphin? The boatman?"

"Yes, Mr. Prime Minister. Dolphin saw the perpetrator of the accident. A small man. At the time he paid no attention— he was just about to check over his boat. Afterwards, he remembered and jumped to the conclusion that he had seen either an obeah-man or a jumbie. I think you should warn the small man to leave Tampica."

Carruthers looked genuinely bewildered. "I have no idea what you are talking about, Mr. Tibbett. I can assure you that at that time we were not suspicious of De Marco or Brinkman. I took it for granted that it was you who—"

"You flatter me too much," said Henry, blandly. Then, "Well, gentlemen, I think the time has come to shake hands on our bargain. We will go into the details later. Meanwhile, I am sure that you would like the first installment of your agreed price. Let us just go over the main points again. In consideration of a payment of two million United States dollars—half a million to be handed over today—you agree to provide unimpeded passage through Tampica, together with storage facilities if necessary, for consignments of marijuana and cocaine, and possibly other similar substances, for nine calendar months. Correct, Mr. Carruthers?"

Carruthers inclined his head.

"I would like your word on it, Mr. Prime Minister."

Reluctantly, Carruthers said, "Yes."

"And you, Mr. Palmer?"

"Yes."

"Good. If you will wait a moment, I'll collect the money. It's upstairs in my room."

Henry got up and walked out. The code word had been given, and the police must even now be moving in on the Anchorage. The plan that he had worked out with the Governor was that the arrests should be made at the moment when the cash was being handed over, thereby giving the police a cast-iron case. He ran up the outside staircase to his bedroom and collected the bulky shopping bags. A quick look inside satisfied him that the contents were intact. Quickly, he came down the steps again and into the dining room.

Carruthers and Palmer did not appear to have moved a muscle since Henry left. They were both trying hard to appear relaxed and at ease, but the strain showed on their faces. In all such transactions, this is the moment of truth.

Henry put the shopping bags on the table, and began taking out the bundles of used notes, which had been secured with elastic bands.

"You can see for yourselves, gentlemen," he said. "Untraceable notes in various denominations, none larger than fifty dollars. Perhaps you would like to count them?"

The other two men were on their feet now, eyes glued greedily to the stack of money on the table. Henry heard a light footstep behind him. Thank God. This was it.

A voice said, "Sit down and put your hands on the table. . . . All of you."

Henry turned. In the doorway of the dining room, with a businesslike gun in his hand, was DEA Agent Wright.

Henry gave him a big grin. "So you came yourself, after all?" He stood up, "Chester Carruthers and Joseph Palmer, as an agent of the C.I.D. I arrest you for—"

Wright said, "Sit down, Tibbett, and put your hands on the table. Okay, Randy. Come in now."

Randy Porter, the young crewman, came in from the garden. He, too, carried a gun. He kicked the dining-room door closed behind him.

"Pack up the money," Wright ordered, "and take it to the boat. I'll finish things here."

Henry sat down slowly, his hands on the table. "You're crazy. The place is crawling with policemen, and every word is being recorded—"

"Wrong on both counts, Tibbett. I disconnected the recorders this morning, while you were down at the dock. The police have been told that the project is postponed, owing to the failure of the recording equipment. All perfectly simple. The Governor believed every word of it. Naturally, he couldn't risk making direct contact with you, but he knows me as a DEA agent. I am above suspicion."

"You *are* a DEA agent," said Henry.

Wright smiled. "True. I have been up to now. Now, I intend to cross to the other side of the road. One of the advantages of my job is that one meets so many interesting people. People with interesting propositions."

Randy Porter had by then repacked the money. Wright made a tiny gesture with his gun. "Okay. Now scram. You know what to do. Get ready for sea and wait for me on board."

Without a word, the boy slipped out of the door and into the garden.

As easily as he could manage, Henry said, "Now what?" He had not liked that remark about finishing things.

"This will take a little time, Tibbett." Wright sounded perfectly relaxed. He glanced at the two black men. "It won't be long now."

Neither Carruthers nor Palmer had said a word since Wright's arrival. Nor had they reacted to Henry's attempted arrest. Now, Henry saw that they were both sitting with hands on the table and eyes closed, breathing heavily. Suddenly, Chester Carruthers slumped forward, insensible.

Wright smiled again. "As the lighter man of the two, the drug takes effect on him more quickly," he explained. As he spoke, the burly Joseph Palmer gave an unhealthy-sounding snort and passed out. "Just nicely timed," Wright added, approvingly.

Henry said, "The women—"

"The women have been dealt with." Wright's light tone was chilling. "And now, Mr. Tibbett, we have a little time to waste, you and I. I don't intend to kill you until just before our two friends here come around." He sat down in Emmy's empty chair. "Let's have a little talk."

14

F or a long moment, the two men looked at each other. Then Henry said, "I could shout for help."

"Certainly you could. But nobody would hear you. On my instructions, all the hotel personnel left as soon as coffee had been served."

"You'll never get away with it."

Wright smiled. "You think not? I don't agree. My plan has the great advantage of simplicity, Mr. Tibbett. It was a simple matter to put the time-release dope in our friends' coffee— Randy did it, as a matter of fact. I had him stationed in the kitchen—as a DEA representative, naturally. By the time Carruthers and Palmer come to, I shall be on my way to South America in *Bellissima*. They will have only the haziest memory of what happened before they passed out. You will be lying here, shot dead, and Carruthers's fingerprints will be all over the gun. It will, of course, come out that you were a British police officer trying to trap the Tampicans into a phony drug deal. Obviously, they blew your cover and killed you. Any way they try to wriggle out of it will simply roll them deeper in the shit." Wright laughed.

"I suppose you've overlooked the fact," said Henry, "that Tampica will no longer be available as a staging post to you and your new masters."

"My dear fellow . . ." Wright was using his mock-

British accent again. "My dear old boy, with Carruthers and Palmer out of the way, the coast is clear."

"What do you mean?"

"Simply that the only other Tampican of sufficient standing to be credibly elected Prime Minister will be Kelly. And Kelly is my creature."

"You can't be sure that the Tampicans will—"

"Oh, yes I can, old boy. The next election is well and truly sewn up, and there's nothing a has-been like Ironmonger can do about it, if that's what you're thinking."

Henry said, "Of course, Agent Stevenson was straight. So he had to go."

"Of course."

"But you didn't kill him, did you?"

"How do you know that?"

"Because I know who did. And I know how you arranged it."

Wright smiled again. "My congratulations, dear fellow. But it won't do you any good or me any harm." He glanced at his watch. "Just a few more minutes. The timing must be right. Sorry to keep you waiting. It must be very tedious."

"It is," Henry assured him.

"Then let's get it over with." Wright stood up, gun in hand.

Behind him, a deep voice said, "Drop that gun before I shoot."

Wright wheeled around in surprise. Lucy Pontefract-Deacon was standing in the open doorway, with a police pistol leveled straight at him. Before he had time to take aim, Lucy fired. Wright gave a shout of pain as his gun dropped from his useless and bleeding right hand.

"I told you to drop it, you silly man." Lucy might have been addressing a naughty dog. "Now sit down. Ah, you have his gun, Henry. Good. Alfred Pendleton and the police will be here soon. I don't think we'll have any more trouble from this—creature."

Henry, who had snatched Wright's gun as it fell, now stood facing Lucy across the table. Both their weapons were trained on Maurice Wright. Henry said, "Where's Emmy? Is she all right?"

"I trust so. I haven't heard from her, of course. That's why I'm here. Your instructions were very precise, as usual, Henry." With a sideways nod of her head, Lucy indicated the two black men. "What happened to Chester and Joe?"

"Agent Wright arranged for them to have a postprandial nap. They'll be coming round soon—just in time for the Commissioner to arrest them."

Wright, who had been nursing his injured hand, said suddenly, "Those won't be the only arrests."

Lucy's eyebrows went up. "No, indeed. You—"

Viciously, Wright said to Henry, "This mad old woman will certainly be arrested for causing grievous bodily harm to an agent of the DEA and obstructing him in his duty. If she has any sense, she will plead lunacy."

"Is the man mad?" Lucy demanded.

"As for you, Tibbett," Wright went on, "I'm afraid a lunacy plea won't get you anywhere. You were explicitly instructed to call off the meeting with Carruthers and Palmer, on account of the malfunctioning of the sound equipment. Instead, you went ahead with it on your own. You drugged the two Tampicans before they could lay hands on the money. Your female accomplice conveniently got the two ladies out of the way, and if I hadn't smelt a rat and come to investigate, you'd have been on your way by now with half a million dollars in your pocket."

"The money will be found on your boat," Henry reminded him.

"Naturally I confiscated the money and had my assistant take it to a place of safety."

"He's a stark raving lunatic."

"Perhaps not quite such a lunatic, Lucy. At least, it's his one hope. If he can bluff this out, he might just be able to avoid being arrested at once, and with *Bellissima* waiting—"

At this moment, two things happened. There was the sound of cars drawing up in the driveway and feet running toward the inn, and Chester Carruthers grunted, sighed, and began to stir in his chair. Suddenly the doorway of the dining room seemed to be full of people. Henry saw the anxious faces of the Governor and the Police Commissioner in the forefront and hovering behind them, half a dozen uniformed policemen looking pardonably puzzled.

"By God, what's going on here?" Pendleton's voice was sharp with a mixture of worry and anger. "Tibbett . . . Wright . . . are you okay?"

Before Henry could speak, Wright said, "Thank God you're here, Sir Alfred." He jumped to his feet. "I got here just in time. I'd have had Tibbett under arrest by now, if this crazy old woman hadn't butted in with a gun."

"My dear fellow." The Governor had noticed Wright's bloodied hand. "You're hurt."

"You bet your sweet life I'm hurt. The old bitch shot the gun out of my hand."

"For heaven's sake, Henry, say something!" Lucy shouted.

"Let him talk," Henry said. "I'll say plenty later."

Joe Palmer was by now beginning to come around, and Carruthers had his eyes open and looked scared stiff.

The Police Commissioner said icily, "For a start, Mr.

Tibbett, and you, Madam, please hand me your weapons."

"With pleasure," said Henry. Lucy glared, but surrendered her gun without more ado.

"Thank you." The Commissioner turned to Sir Alfred. "And now, sir, if I may suggest it, I think we should all adjourn to headquarters and thrash this matter out. I shall need to take statements from all here present."

Henry said to Wright, "Where's my wife? Where are Mrs. Palmer and Mrs. Carruthers?"

With a savage smile, Wright said, "You should know. I haven't set eyes on them."

Henry appealed to the Governor, "Sir, these three ladies have been abducted and possibly harmed."

"For heaven's sake, Tibbett, we'll find them soon enough. Sergeant, Constable—get these people to police headquarters at once."

The Priest Town Police Station had none of the dreary grimness associated with such establishments in more northerly climes. It was a low whitewashed building set among gardens of hibiscus and oleander, and the afternoon sunshine poked lazy fingers of light through the louvered windows of the Commissioner's office.

Henry had to wait, fuming with impatience, while the Governor and the Commissioner listened to Wright's account. At last, he himself was sitting on the hard chair facing the big desk, where Sir Alfred was fiddling with a sheaf of papers. There was no sign of the Commissioner.

Henry began at once. "Sir, my wife and those other two women—"

"Now, don't fuss, Tibbett. Commissioner Ramsay is following up on the search at this very moment. You and I have other things to talk about."

"Many things," agreed Henry dryly.

Sir Alfred did not appear to hear him. He went on, "Wright has told me an extraordinary story, Tibbett."

"I know it, sir."

"For a start, you must admit that his credentials are absolutely in order. Everything has been checked with Washington. Agent Wright is a valued member of the Drug Enforcement Agency."

"Was," said Henry.

"So was Agent Stevenson, who lost his life in the course of duty. Let's have no argument about that."

Henry said nothing.

The Governor went on. "Now, you surely must know that yesterday afternoon Wright called me to report that the electronic recording system that we'd had installed at the Anchorage was malfunctioning. I don't have to tell you that without proper taped evidence, we could never get a conviction against these men. We are, after all, dealing with the Prime Minister and Finance Minister of a sovereign and friendly power. The case against them has to be completely watertight. Wright informed me that you had agreed with him to abort the meeting for the time being. You were supposed to telephone Tampica and cancel the arrangements."

"None of that is true, sir."

"I myself called off the planned police raid on the Anchorage. The next thing I heard was this afternoon—an extraordinary message from Lucy Pontefract-Deacon that Commissioner Ramsay and I should come to St. Matthews and to the Anchorage as soon as possible, as a very dangerous situation had arisen. I have the high-speed police launch at my disposal, so we were able to arrive within the hour."

"Have you spoken to Lucy?" Henry asked.

For the first time, Pendleton permitted himself the ghost of a smile. "I would say, rather, that Lucy has spoken to me.

185

Or shouted at me, to be accurate. Naturally, she refuses to hear a word against you. Nevertheless, she admits that she received her so-called instructions in the form of a typewritten note pushed through her mailbox yesterday afternoon. It was unsigned, but purported to come from you. She assumed that it had been delivered by a messenger from Pirate's Cave Hotel—apparently she had told you to entrust messages for her to the manager there."

Pendleton looked inquiringly at Henry, who said nothing. He went on. "The note told her to come to St. Mark's on the night ferry, and from here to St. Matthew's on the connecting boat. She was to take a room at a small hotel in Priest Town. She was to bring with her the pistol that she is legally permitted to keep for her own protection, since she lives in an isolated area. If she did not receive a reassuring phone call from Mrs. Tibbett by three o'clock, she was to get an urgent message to me and come to the Anchorage herself, armed. The note hinted that she would find you in need of help. Finally, she was instructed to burn the note, which she did.

"What she found at the Anchorage—and she freely admits this—was the two Tampicans lying drugged in their chairs at the dining table, and Agent Wright covering you with his gun. Acting on a very unfortunate impulse, she shot the gun out of his hand—which puts her in an awkward position, legally. She says that you then grabbed Wright's gun, and the two of you held him until we arrived. There is no dispute about any of this.

"Incidentally, my men found the cash on Agent Wright's boat, just as he said we would. It was taken there by Wright's young assistant, Porter. Wright alleges that when he arrived at the Anchorage, the money was loose on the table, the Tampicans were already drugged, and you were preparing to make off with the cash." Sir Alfred cleared his throat. "And there's another thing, Tibbett."

"Another? Isn't that enough?"

"Some years ago . . ." Sir Alfred was clearly embarrassed, and cleared his throat again. "Some years ago, as you must remember, Tibbett, there was an episode involving drugs in the British Seawards. You were very much a part of that."

"But—"

Sir Alfred silenced him with a gesture. "Oh, I know that your involvement with drugs was involuntary, and we all felt that you did the Seawards a great service. Nevertheless, I have to remind you that you were on drugs at one time, and that your behavior was such that I had to sign a deportation order against you, and that the chief miscreants were never caught, although smaller fry were prosecuted."

For a moment, Henry was speechless. Then he said, angrily, "How can you possibly insinuate such things? You know perfectly well that I was deliberately drugged."

"I know, I know, my dear fellow. But once a man has experimented with these dangerous substances, whether by his own intention or not, there is a tendency, as Agent Wright pointed out—"

"So he even found out about that incident, did he? He certainly did his homework. Now, sir, shall I tell you about Agent Maurice Wright?"

Pendleton leaned back in his chair. "I wish you would, Tibbett." He did not sound unfriendly.

"It's perfectly true," Henry began, "that Agent Wright is an accredited member of the DEA. He and Agent Stevenson were sent to Tampica to lay a trap for Carruthers and Palmer. Stevenson was a perfectly upright and honest officer. That's why he was killed."

187

"By Wright?"

"No," said Henry. "Not directly. I'll come to that later. When Wright came and told me he was an undercover DEA man I believed him. I had to, in view of his credentials, not only from Washington but from you yourself, sir. Of course I agreed to cooperate with him in every way. It was only later that I became suspicious. Still, there was nothing I could do. I had no hard evidence, just my—well, a sort of instinct. I just hoped that his plan had misfired and that he would go away. When he turned up here in the Seawards just before we were due to make our arrests, I became convinced that he was . . . what I thought he was."

"And what was that?"

"A turncoat. A bent policeman. As he himself remarked to me, in his profession he meets so many interesting people. Like drug barons, multimillionaires who could offer him more for an hour's betrayal of his superiors' trust than he could earn in a couple of years. In a curious way, I can see his point of view. I wonder why there aren't more like him."

"So what do you think was Wright's plan?"

"I don't think, sir. I know. He was kind enough to explain it to me in detail, while we were waiting."

"Waiting for what?"

"For him to kill me."

"Really, Tibbett, I think that calls for some elaboration."

Henry elaborated. Then he went on, "It was a simple and ingenious scheme. All the more so when you consider that his original plan had had to be abandoned."

"His original plan?"

"Oh, yes. Wright was planning to arrest Carruthers and Palmer, thus leaving the way open for the election of Kelly as Prime Minister. He would have stayed on with the DEA,

188

double-crossing them all the time for his own benefit and that of his new employers. As it was, my arrival and the death of Stevenson—or should I say, the necessity for Stevenson's death—changed everything. Under the new scheme, Wright and Porter would have disappeared with the money, and the DEA would have been after him, but on the other hand, my death would have been pinned fair and square on Carruthers and Palmer, so the safe passage of drugs through Tampica would have been assured. There remained only the question of what to do with Emmy. Now do you understand why I'm so worried?"

Sir Alfred scratched his chin. "This is the damnedest situation I've ever known," he said. "Two top-ranking plain-clothes officers each accusing the other of treachery. And both of you putting up pretty good stories, at that."

"What possible reason," Henry demanded, "did Wright give for coming back here and interfering with our operation, when he had agreed to stay out of it?"

"Surely you can guess, Tibbett. Because he was suspicious of you. And then you demanded all that money in cash. His idea was to tell you to abort the meeting. He would then go and check up on whether you had obeyed instructions. It's clear that you had not."

"Because I never received any. If I had, don't you think that I would have double-checked with you, Sir Alfred?"

The Governor shook his head. "I just don't know, Tibbett."

"I suppose you told him about the money," added Henry bitterly.

"He was with me when you telephoned," said Pendleton, simply. "It did seem to confirm his suspicions."

15

Emmy was finding her garden tour with Emmalinda and Carmelita somewhat hard going. Carmelita had lost a lot of the gaiety and easy sophistication she had shown over lunch and was mooching around the Anchorage gardens, evincing minimal interest in the floral beauties there. And why should she be interested, Emmy reflected, when she herself lived in the horticultural paradise of The Lodge in Tampica? Once or twice, Carmelita glanced at her watch, as if impatient for this boring jaunt to be over.

As for Emmalinda, hers was a different case. Emmy had noticed that the older woman had done herself proud on the rum punches before lunch and the wine during the meal, and she now appeared definitely unsteady on her feet and woozy in her general outlook. Not an easy couple of guests.

However, Emmy had promised Henry that she would keep them occupied and as far as possible away from the inn itself until at least a quarter to three. If by then the police had arrived and the party exploded into a shambles of arrests, Emmy knew that she must put through a call to the hotel in Priest Town, where Lucy would be waiting for a news bulletin. This was a result of the telephone call that Henry had had her make to Patrick Bishop at Pirate's Cave the evening before, asking him to arrange for certain instructions to be conveyed to Lucy. Henry had not confided in Emmy the exact reason for this odd setup, but Emmy was quite used to obeying orders she did not understand. It was all part of being Henry's wife.

"Our friends the Colvilles, who used to own the Anchorage," she heard herself saying, "did a lot of grafting. Look at this hibiscus—single yellow and triple red flowers all in bloom together on a basic red stock."

She hadn't really expected it to go over big, and it didn't. Carmelita yawned and looked at her watch again. Emmalinda swayed slightly and muttered something about sitting down. It was with the emotion of a shipwrecked mariner who spots a sail on the horizon that Emmy saw a young man hurrying across the lawn toward her, and recognized Randy Porter, Agent Wright's young crewman.

Her feeling of relief was momentarily replaced by alarm. Had either Carmelita or Emmalinda seen Randy in Tampica, and would they associate him with Agent Wright? But neither showed any signs of recognition. Carmelita turned away to inspect the grafted hibiscus, while Emmalinda had discovered a garden seat, collapsed onto it, and was merely wiping her face with a huge red handkerchief.

"Ah, there you are, Mrs. Tibbett." Randy sounded harassed. "I have a message from your husband. For you and these two ladies."

"Oh, yes?" Emmy was still a little uneasy.

"The fact is, their business is taking longer than they expected. Mr. Carruthers and Mr. Palmer suggest that their wives should go down to the ferryboat and wait for them there. And Sir Alfred Pendleton is at the Golf Club and would be glad if you, Mrs. Tibbett, would join him for a cup of coffee. I can take you all in my Jeep."

191

Emmy looked at her watch. It was shortly after two o'clock. "I have to be back here by a quarter to three," she said. "I've a phone call to make."

Randy smiled. "Of course. Plenty of time. Or you can make your call from the Golf Club."

Carmelita turned around. "Let's go," she said, shortly. "Come along, Emmalinda." She and Porter helped Mrs. Palmer to her feet, and the four of them made their way to the hired Jeep standing in the yard of the Anchorage.

Emmy and Carmelita climbed into the backseat, and Randy, with a certain amount of difficulty, managed to heave Emmalinda onto the passenger seat beside him.

"Right," he said cheerfully. "First stop, the jetty."

The ferryboat was tied up alongside the stone wharf, but since it was almost an hour to sailing time, there were few people about. Porter jumped out of the Jeep, and Carmelita quickly followed him, clambering easily over the front seat. Between them, they helped Mrs. Palmer down.

"Will you be all right, Mrs. Carruthers?" Randy sounded anxious. "Can you manage?"

Carmelita seemed to have recovered her good spirits. "I'll be fine," she said. "I'll just help her down to the boat." She gave Randy and Emmy a wicked little wink. "Poor Emmalinda. I'm afraid the heat's a bit much for her. Best let her sleep it off."

"Very well then, Mrs. Carruthers. Have a good trip home." Obviously relieved, Porter got back into the Jeep and swept it in a tight U-turn back onto the road toward the Golf Club.

Tentatively, Emmy said, "I saw the *Bellissima* was in, but I didn't know that you and . . . that is . . ."

Randy grinned. "Agent Wright and I," he said, "are still on the job, even if unofficially."

"So you know—"

"Of course. I'm not DEA myself, but I help when I can. We thought your husband might need us."

Emmy relaxed. "I'm certainly glad you're here," she said. "How's it going back at the Anchorage?"

"Okay, but slowly. Agent Wright may have to move to help Mr. Tibbett. That's why he—"

"Just a moment." Emmy was no longer relaxed. "This isn't the way to the Golf Club."

"Back entrance, Mrs. Tibbett. Sir Alfred thought it would be better."

"Why on earth should he think that? And why does he want to see me?"

"Search me," said Randy, with an attractive grin. "I'm just the errand boy around here." He drove for some time in silence then he remarked, "Ah, here we are."

The Jeep had pulled up at a small wooden building like a bus-stop shelter, which stood beside a large pair of slatted gates, presumably leading to the gardens of the Golf Club. There was nobody to be seen.

"Out you get," Randy went on. "I'll just park the Jeep and be back to take you in. Shan't be many minutes."

After five minutes of sitting on the hard bench in the hut, Emmy began to feel both cross and apprehensive. She got up and inspected the gates. They were padlocked and topped with barbed wire, as was the stout wire fence on either side of them. She looked at her watch: 2:30. This was ridiculous. She had to get back to the Anchorage. Where was Porter and what was he playing at? She looked up and down the empty road. The shrill call of a thrasher bird mocked her. Otherwise, silence.

Exasperation turned to anger. She had deliberately been taken from the Anchorage and dumped in this God-forsaken spot. But why? Suddenly, she heard the sound of an engine. A car was bowling along the road toward her in the direction of Priest Town—not a Jeep but a closed sedan. She ran into the road and waved her arms to hail it.

It was not necessary. The car was already pulling up beside her, and to her amazement, Emmy saw that the driver was Carmelita Carruthers. She leaned in through the open window.

"Hi, there, Carmelita. What on earth is happening?"

Without ceremony, Carmelita said, "Get in."

"I still want to know—"

"Don't waste time. Get in."

"Well . . ." Emmy hesitated, then opened the door and got in beside the driver. After all, anything was better than being stuck on a deserted country road, and she had to get back to the Anchorage, which lay on the far side of Priest Town. Her watch read 2:40.

The car door had barely closed when Carmelita stepped on the accelerator with a savage stab of her foot, and the car shot off like a bullet.

Somewhat embarrassed, Emmy said, "Can you be very kind and drive me straight to the Anchorage? I have to—"

"Never you mind where you're going." Carmelita sounded quite calm, but with an undertone of pure steel. Her slim hands with their crimson-painted talons of fingernails suddenly whirled the wheel to the left, and the car bumped down a rutted track that Emmy could see led to the ocean.

"I have to go to the Anchorage," she repeated.

Carmelita did not reply. She was driving the car much too fast over the corrugations of dried mud. Soon the track petered out as it entered a plantation of coco palms, and the sandy ground obliterated the path. However, Emmy could see the tire marks of other vehicles that crisscrossed among the trees. In another minute, the car stopped on the edge of the beach, which bordered a small, crescent-shaped bay, like so many others on the island. A rubber dinghy was pulled up onto the coral sand, and a small white sailboat rode quietly at anchor in the center of the bay. She was a small cabin cruiser, about twenty feet long and sloop-rigged. Her mainsail was furled along the boom and secured by tiers, ready to be hoisted, and her jib was wrapped around the forestay, only waiting for a tug from the cockpit to release the swivel mechanism. There was no other boat in sight, nor any sign of another human being.

Carmelita switched off the car engine and said, "Get out."

"But—"

"I said get out." Emmy felt something cold and hard digging into her ribs. Carmelita had produced a small but efficient-looking gun, which she was pressing against Emmy's body. "No questions, or I shoot."

"This is ridiculous." Emmy attempted a laugh, but it was unconvincing. "What on earth are you playing at, Mrs. Carruthers?"

"No playing. Get out." Carmelita reached across Emmy with her free hand and opened the passenger door. Then she gave Emmy a very firm shove in the ribs with the gun. Emmy got out.

"Good." Carmelita jumped out of the car, still keeping her weapon trained on Emmy. "Now the dinghy. We go on board."

A sudden spurt of anger obscured Emmy's fear. "You wouldn't dare shoot me," she said. "And I'm bigger and stronger than you are. Get out of my way. I'm going to drive back to the Anchorage."

She took a step toward the black girl, and there was a

sudden, crisp sound, like a firecracker. Emmy cried out, and bent to clutch her left leg. Carmelita smiled.

"You thought I wouldn't shoot? You are very silly, Mrs. Tibbett. I am an excellent shot, and if I wanted to kill you, I could do so very easily. As it is, your leg will not be too troublesome. Get in the dinghy."

For a moment Emmy looked straight at Carmelita. Then she limped toward the dinghy. Dimly, certain things were beginning to become clear, and she had at least an inkling of what was happening. For the moment, there was nothing to do but to get into the dinghy and board the sailboat.

Carmelita said, "Wait. I'll help you."

Emmy's leg was beginning to hurt badly, but she realized that the damage was only a flesh wound in the calf, and that the leg was still operational. She stopped gratefully beside the rubber boat and took a headscarf from her bag, with which she bandaged her leg. Carmelita, much stronger than she looked, was dragging the dinghy down the beach and into the softly breaking wavelets at the edge of the sea. She nodded approvingly.

"That's right. Bind it up tight. Now get in."

As Emmy managed to clamber into the flimsy craft and seat herself on one of the wooden thwarts, Carmelita gave the dinghy a final push out to send it offshore toward the yacht, as she herself jumped as nimbly as a cat over the bows and picked up an oar to use as a paddle. Seconds later, the dinghy was bumping alongside the sailboat: Carmelita secured the painter around a shroud, jumped aboard, and held out a hand for Emmy to grasp.

"Pull yourself up. Okay. Get your right foot on deck—good—there!" Emmy found herself deposited in a heap on the deck. Her leg was now hurting abominably. Carmelita said, "Not bad, considering you know nothing about boats."

With a surge of relief, Emmy remembered her chance and inaccurate remark at the Palmers' lunch. She resolved to know even less about boats in the immediate future.

Carmelita gave her a hand to help her up from the deck, and then propelled her down the companionway and into the tiny cabin. "Sit there." She pushed Emmy down onto one of the bunks. "Okay. You stay there. He will come with more instructions."

"Who is he?"

"You'll find out."

"Where is my husband?"

"I don't think you will be seeing your husband again," said Carmelita, tersely. She scaled the companion ladder, lithe as a ballet dancer, and Emmy heard the soft splash of the paddle as the dinghy made its way ashore again. Then the car engine started up and, after a couple of noisy reverses, faded as it made its way back to the road. After that, silence.

It would not be accurate to say that Emmy's brain raced brilliantly to come up with a complete explanation of the events of the past hour. However, certain basic facts were obvious. Carmelita was hand-in-glove with the mysterious "him," the man who had supplied her with cocaine in Dr. Duncan's clinic, and who now appeared to be involved in some sort of conspiracy, not only against Henry and the Seawards government, but also against Carmelita's own husband and his colleagues.

It is a tribute to Maurice Wright's ability for deception, or perhaps to Emmy's instinctive belief in the sanctity of law and order and its guardians, that it never occurred to her for a moment to suspect him. Her thoughts turned to Police Commissioner Kelly, to Patrick Bishop of Pirate's Cave, even—for a fleeting, guilty moment—to Sir Edward Iron-monger himself. For one thing she was profoundly grateful: she had not telephoned Lucy, so that stalwart lady would have realized by now that something was wrong, and taken action. This gave Emmy hope for Henry and his survival.

She dismissed Carmelita's role in the proceedings with an angry shrug. The girl was a hopeless addict and would do anything to ensure her next fix. So much for her. Randy Porter, Emmy was inclined to consider as no more than a guileless young adventurer. He had probably been paid to carry out some inexplicable but apparently harmless actions—like pretending to take her to the Golf Club and then abandoning her. Emmy hoped that he would not find himself in trouble or danger as a result.

Meanwhile, she secured the makeshift bandage on her leg with a safety pin from the boat's first-aid box, and stood up gingerly. To her relief, she found that, although painful and stiffening rapidly, her leg was not useless. She could still move around, though with difficulty. However, there was no question of being able to swim ashore—and even if she had done so, how could she find transport on that lonely road? There was only one thing to be done. The boat was ready for sea and, since she had no motor, Emmy would have to sail her to Priest Town Harbour. She certainly had no intention of sitting there like a bump on a log, as one of her American friends had put it, until "he" arrived.

The first difficulty was that Emmy had no clear idea of where she was. She tried to remember the routes of her drives with Randy and Carmelita. Randy had left the Priest Town jetty on the road toward the Golf Club, which meant along the shore toward the west. Then the Jeep had turned left, or inland, but was still heading west and slightly south.

Emmy considered. It was not possible, she decided, that the gate where Randy had dropped her was a back entrance to the Golf Club. They must have long since passed the Club's compound and been well to the west of it. Then Carmelita had appeared from the opposite direction, driving east, and had quickly turned left toward the sea. If that was so, Priest Town should lie a few miles to the east-northeast, with the Golf Club even closer. The only snag was that as the prevailing trade winds blew steadily from the northeast, it would be a dead beat to windward to get back to the harbor. Couldn't be helped. Stiffly, Emmy climbed into the cockpit.

Luckily the little yacht—her name was *Dolly Bird*—was equipped with modern gear to make the handling of the sails easy. Not so luckily, she was not designed for singlehanded sailing, for not all the lines ran back into the cockpit. Emmy realized that to hoist the mainsail she would have to scramble up onto the cabin roof. The wind was light, and beating under jib alone she would never reach Priest Town before dark. Then there was the anchor. No fancy gadgets like electric winches operated from the cockpit. She would just have to go forward and pull.

First things first. The mainsail. Emmy freed the mainsheet, then climbed painfully out of the cockpit and onto the deck, steadying herself by holding on to the shrouds. Avoiding the swinging boom, she reached the mast, and squinting up against the sun, disentangled the main halyard from the other rigging lines and began hauling on it. The mainsail came up sweetly, and Emmy's heart with it. With the big sail flapping idly, she went back to the cockpit and unfurled the jib. She knew that she must have maximum sail power available at the moment when the anchor came up.

She sheeted the mainsail in loosely on the port side—that is, the starboard tack—but the jib she sheeted on the starboard side, so that the boat would fall off to port, and offshore, when the anchor came up. Then, hoping that there was not too much heavy chain between the end of the warp and the anchor itself, she clambered back up to the bows and began to pull.

The first few yards of anchor warp came up easily enough, and *Dolly Bird* rode forward as she was pulled up over the anchor; but then, even before the first link of the chain was out of the water, Emmy was thrown backward, with an agonizing wrench of her injured leg. The anchor was either fouled or so heavy as to be immovable without a winch or a strong masculine crew.

Emmy got to her feet and pulled again until her arms ached. Then she lay down on the deck and gazed over the bow into the clear water below, and at once she saw what had happened. Beneath *Dolly Bird*'s hull there was a cluster of rocks into which the anchor chain disappeared. The anchor was foul of the rocks, and only a diver could free it. Emmy breathed a mental apology to the unknown owner, and went aft to look for a knife.

In the drawer under the small gas-burning stove, Emmy found a strong serrated-edge kitchen knife. Armed with it, she made another agonizing scramble up to the bows, and in a matter of seconds, the anchor warp was cut through. Then, a dash back to the cockpit to free the jibsheet as the sails filled on the starboard tack. Jibsheet hauled in on the port side, helm adjusted—and *Dolly Bird* was sailing, wind abeam, away from the beach. Thankful for the small stainless-steel sheet winches, Emmy sheeted in the sails and put the helm up to windward. Now the boat was beating on the starboard tack, making progress up the coast as well as out to sea. Emmy settled back in the cockpit, her hand on the helm, and took stock of her situation.

It was not desperate, she reckoned, but not very encouraging either. She was without motor or anchor. She was beating up a coast she didn't know, not absolutely certain that she was even going in the right direction. One reassuring fact was that she was moving quickly away from the little bay where "he" was expected. Indeed, after no more than ten minutes, she was able to bring the boat about to the port tack and clear the little headland that had sheltered her original anchorage. Out of sight, then. But out of mind? That was another story.

Once the headland was safely astern, Emmy came about again, heading out to sea. She lashed the helm with the fall of the mainsheet, and went below. Surely there must be a chart of the entrance to Priest Town Harbour, and she needed it badly. To go onto the rocks at this stage would be ridiculous.

It took some searching, but there was a chart. Emmy grabbed it and made her way back up into the cockpit. The little boat was holding her course nicely, east-northeast and away from the shore. With great relief, Emmy recognized the Golf Club beach coming up on her starboard bow. Now she knew for sure where she was.

The chart showed that she had been right to get a good offing from the shore. Treacherous rocks marched out from the coast between the Golf Club and Priest Town Harbour, and to make the entrance—which was clearly marked with red-and-green buoys—even a shallow-draught boat must stand off at least a mile before making the turn to starboard that would bring it through the marked entrance on a comfortable beam wind. Emmy realized that she would have to stay on her present course for quite a while. She looked at her watch: 4:10. How could so much have happened in such a short time? Anyhow, what mattered now was to make sufficient offing to clear the entrance to the harbor before the tropical dusk fell with its incredible speed, turning a bright sunset to complete darkness in a matter of minutes.

As *Dolly Bird* clawed her way up the coast, Emmy could see a few other boats making their way back to harbor before darkness fell. Small day-sailers from the Golf Club were scudding inshore through the buoyed channel through the reef; further ahead, larger sailing yachts had taken down their sails and were motoring in toward Priest Town Harbour. Lucky devils, thought Emmy. I'll never be snobbish about not having a motor on a sailboat again. Then she heard, faintly, the sound of an engine astern of her.

Looking back over her shoulder, she saw the shape of a small powerboat overtaking her from behind. Her first emotion was one of relief. Perhaps he'll give me a tow into Priest Town. She waved a hopeful arm as the motorboat drew closer. No, not really a motorboat. She could see it now: it was a large dinghy, powered by a big outboard engine. In it, one person. Closer still now, and she recognized the boat and its occupant. It was *Bellissima*'s dinghy, driven by Randy Porter.

Emmy had no means of knowing whether the boy's intentions were friendly or deadly, but she decided to take no chances. At the moment, her course was taking her farther and farther out to sea, away from the friendly coast, the other boats, the Golf Club moorings. Her very last wish was to end up at the Golf Club jetty, an unwelcome outsider with endless explanations before she could get to Henry and the Anchorage. But there was nothing for it. She put the helm up and came about.

Now, on the port tack, she was making a good course for the first of the Golf Club buoys. With immense relief, she realized that she could make the entrance. Inside the protected Golf Club anchorage, she was prepared to talk to Randy Porter; not outside on the open sea.

It did not take long for Porter to catch up with her. He roared the whaler up to within hailing distance and shouted, "Mrs. Tibbett! Mrs. Tibbett!"

Emmy ignored him, holding her course. Again he called, "Mrs. Tibbett! Please heave to! I have news for you. I have to come aboard!"

"See you at the Golf Club," Emmy shouted back.

Randy did not reply. Instead there was a sharp report, and something whistled across *Dolly Bird*'s bows, ricocheting along the water. Emmy almost laughed. How often had she heard the phrase "a shot across the bows." Now it had actually happened. Porter was determined not to let her get into harbor.

Emmy looked around. Where were the comforting little boats that had been sailing up the channel to the Golf Club? Twilight was falling fast, and she knew very well where they were—safely inside the reef and tied up to the jetty or hauled up on the beach. Out here, in the deepening dusk, there were only two boats. Steadfastly she held her course—the course that would take her between the red-and-green buoys and into the safe haven of the Golf Club.

Porter opened up the big outboard engine so that it roared powerfully. As the dinghy sped across her bows, she saw the gun in his hand and ducked just in time, as the bullet thudded into the cockpit coaming. To think that she had actually felt worried about this young thug. She crouched on the deck of the cockpit, reaching up to the tiller to keep the boat on course. Once again the motor thundered closer, and another shot tore a hole on the foot of the mainsail.

Emmy knew that she could not keep her head down within the protective sides of the cockpit much longer. She could not see the compass and was having to steer purely on the behavior of the sails. As she knew, the wind was likely to shift as she came under the lee of the land. If she lost her course now, she would end up on the reef, crippled and helpless. She risked raising her head for a brief moment and saw that she was pointing up too far and would soon be out of the channel. She corrected course and ducked down again, just in time.

And then came what seemed to Emmy the most beautiful sound in the world. A second engine, with a steady purr that was softer but just as potent as Porter's outboard. It grew louder, and a reassuring voice called, "Ahoy there! *Dolly Bird*, ahoy! Everyt'ing okay dere?"

Emmy jumped up and waved. "Dolphin! What are you doing here?"

"Miz Tibbett! You okay?"

"Not really, Dolphin. I've hurt my leg, and—"

"T'row me a line if you can, Miz Tibbett. I tow you in. You can get dem sails off of her?"

"Oh, yes. Of course I can." Emmy put the nose of the boat up into the wind and furled the flapping jib. She scrambled onto the deck, paused at the mast to drop the mainsail, which fell onto the deck in a crumpled mass of white nylon, and went up to the bows. The anchor warp, which she had cut loose in what seemed like another lifetime, made a satisfactory towrope. Dolphin caught it expertly and put his motor slow ahead, so that *Dolly Bird* was eased gently onto course and toward the harbor. In the distance, Emmy saw *Bellissima's* dinghy streaking westward into the sunset, until it rounded the first headland and went out of sight.

It was all over but the shouting.

16

And there was no lack of shouting. From the Golf Club, Emmy telephoned the police station and was immensely relieved to be told that Henry was there, alive and well; however, her relief turned to incredulous anger when it became obvious that he was under suspicion of some sort. She threatened to call the Governor immediately, and was told that he, too, was on the premises. At her urgent insistence, she was put through to Sir Alfred Pendleton.

"Mrs. Tibbett! Where are you? We've all been extremely worried about you."

"No more than I've been," Emmy assured him. "I've been kidnapped and shot in the leg and—however, none of that matters. I'm okay and I'm at the Golf Club. What you've got to do now is get after Randy Porter and Carmelita Carruthers. Try the *Bellissima*—Agent Wright's boat. She's anchored in a cove a few miles west of the Golf Club, unless she's already made a run for it. At least, that's the direction her dinghy came from. She can't be far away."

"Just what are you accusing Mrs. Carruthers and Mr. Porter of doing, Mrs. Tibbett?"

"She kidnapped me and shot me in the leg, and he's been trying to kill me. Is that enough?"

"But why, Mrs. Tibbett?"

"I have absolutely no idea, Sir Alfred. Perhaps Henry can tell you. He never tells me anything. Now, for heaven's sake get after them. Oh, and another thing, I think Agent Wright may be in danger. If he's on that boat—"

"He is not on the boat, Mrs. Tibbett. As for being in danger, that rather depends how you look at it. Now, get your leg seen to and come over here as fast as you can."

The Golf Club secretary, who looked more like a distinguished member of the United States Senate than most senators do, took everything in his unflappable stride. The club employed a resident nurse, and in a very short time Emmy's leg had been expertly treated and her general health protected by an antitetanus shot and antibiotics.

While waiting for the taxi that was to take her to the police station, Emmy was able to unravel the mystery of how Dolphin had appeared in his parasailing towboat at the crucial moment. His temporary job at the Golf Club was explained, and also the fact that *Dolly Bird* was a private boat belonging to a club member, who kept her in the club's marina to sail when he visited the island. She had disappeared sometime during the previous night, and a general watch was being kept for her. Dolphin was snugging down his boat and equipment for the evening, when he spotted *Dolly Bird* under sail and heading on a somewhat wavering course for the club—but apparently with nobody at the helm. Naturally, he had gone out to investigate.

"Thank God you did, Dolphin," said Emmy. "I'll never know how to thank you. You saved my life."

"Mr. Henry, he save mine," said Dolphin simply. He reached out and took Emmy's hand. "My mother say he big obeah-man. That not so. He big commonsense man. He okay?"

Emmy put her other hand over Dolphin's large black one. "He's okay, Dolphin. He's also quite mad."

"He good man."

Emmy smiled. "Yes, you're right. Good but quite mad."

"Mrs. Tibbett, your taxi is here." A trim coffee-colored receptionist was looking at the pair of them disapprovingly from behind her high desk, implying that the reception area was hardly a fitting place for a mere boatman. Impulsively, Emmy leaned forward and kissed Dolphin's cheek. Then she hurried toward the heavily barred gate, where the taxi was waiting.

At the police station, Emmy was ushered into the small room that had become the Governor's temporary office. Henry was there, looking tired but considerably relieved, and Sir Alfred was talking on the telephone.

"Good. Very good work, Sergeant. Yes, straight to St. Mark's. Come back tomorrow morning for me and the rest of our"—he hesitated—"our visitors." He put down the telephone. "Well, we caught them. *Bellissima* was upping her anchor and preparing to sneak off without lights. The police launch is taking the prisoners over to St. Mark's now." Sir Alfred looked at Henry and Emmy, shook his head, smiling, and said, "My God, I hope never to see you two on my territory again. For heaven's sake, what is going on?"

"Ask him," said Emmy, with a touch of mutiny.

"Oh, dear," Henry said. "It's a long story." With an abrupt change of tone, he added, "Where's Lucy?"

"Right here," said Pendleton. "In the next room."

"And Carruthers and Palmer?"

"Settling in for a night at the Golf Club at government expense." Sir Alfred threw up his hands. "What else could I do? Mrs. Palmer is there, too. Seems she was given a dose of the same drug, but has now recovered."

Pendleton glared at Henry and Emmy. "Now, for God's

sake, tell me what's happening. Or am I always to be the last to know?"

Before Henry could answer, Emmy said, "By the way, what about Agent Wright?"

"He's under arrest," Henry said.

"Agent Wright is?" Emmy was dumbfounded.

The Governor looked at his watch. He said, "This is obviously going to take a lot of explaining. I suggest we collect Lucy and all go to the Anchorage for a drink and something to eat."

Henry found it hard to believe that the four of them were sitting at the same pink-clothed table at which he and Emmy had lunched only a few hours earlier, and yet a lifetime away.

"What put you onto Wright in the first place?" Emmy was asking.

"It was when I realized that Carmelita Carruthers had arranged for Stevenson's accident by sabotaging Dolphin's boat."

"She couldn't have," Lucy objected. "She was at Dr. Duncan's clinic in St. Mark's. I took her there myself."

"That's what we all thought," Henry agreed, "but Dolphin's description of the person he saw on the beach somehow stuck in my mind. 'A small man'—that is, a slim man—and 'with blood on his hands and feet.' At first I thought the bit about the blood was just hysterical imagination; but then it occurred to me that the 'small man' might have been a woman wearing jeans. Dolphin only got a glimpse of the figure, and the light wasn't good."

"And the blood was Carmelitas nail varnish!" exclaimed Lucy triumphantly.

"That's right. She was the only black woman I saw on

209

Tampica who used that bright red varnish. The fashionable thing seems to be gold or silver, like Ilicia at the airport." Henry paused. "But if it was Carmelita that Dolphin saw, how did she come to be in Tampica instead of St. Mark's? And why would she want to harm Agent Stevenson? Surely not because he had refused to give her a fix? No, it had to be a tradeoff. Somebody smuggled cocaine to her in the clinic and got her back to Tampica, in return for tampering with Dolphin's boat. Well, then, who knew where Carmelita was?"

"Nobody but me." Lucy was very firm.

"That's where you're wrong, Lucy. Wright knew, and he was foolish enough to mention it to Sir Alfred and myself." He smiled at Lucy. "Just think back, Lucy. How hard did you have to persuade Carmelita to go with you to Dr. Duncan's clinic?"

Emmy would not have thought it possible that Lucy Pontefract-Deacon could blush, but a deeper color crept into her tanned face. "I didn't have to persuade her at all. She suggested it."

"Didn't that surprise you?"

"Yes, it did. Surprised and delighted me. When I told you, Emmy, that I had persuaded her to go there, it wasn't exactly an untruth. I'd been trying to get her there for months, and I thought that she'd finally come to her senses."

Henry nodded. "That's the piece of the jigsaw that I was missing. Agent Stevenson's so-called accident was carefully worked out in advance by Wright and Carmelita. Of course, he had been supplying her with cocaine all along. That is, supplying it and withholding it when he wanted her help. She was completely in his power. So when he found out who I was, he gave her the necessary instructions."

"What instructions?" Pendleton wanted to know.

"First, to approach Stevenson for a fix of the white girl, which he knew would be refused. Then to visit Lucy and go with her to Duncan's clinic on St. Mark's—where, of course, a fix was supplied. As you may know, Doc Duncan doesn't believe in keeping patients in his clinic by force. She was perfectly free to leave the following evening, which she did. *Bellissima* was waiting to bring her back to Tampica overnight so that she could tamper with Dolphin's boat in the morning and apparently have a perfect alibi. Wright made another mistake when he tried to make me believe that it would take far longer than it actually did to get from Tampica to St. Mark's in *Bellissima*. Anyhow, Carmelita flew back to the Seawards on the early plane that same day, and slipped back into the clinic. She left again that evening and got to the airport in time to waylay Emmy."

"Ilicia Murphy at the airport—" Emmy began.

"A very important young lady," said Henry. "I think she was acting quite innocently, but that doesn't mean that she didn't do a lot of harm. Wright must have told her his identity as a DEA agent and asked her to supply him with certain information. And another thing—why did Sir Edward drop Emmy so far from the airport? He made it sound like a prudent precaution, but, thinking it over, it didn't make much sense. After all, Emmy and I had met him quite openly at Pirate's Cave and proclaimed ourselves old acquaintances. I decided there must be somebody at the airport—somebody whom Ironmonger *knew* would be there, which means an employee—whom he did not wish to meet just then. And another small mystery—what was his connection with Melinda's Market? Why did he choose it of all places to accept his most private phone calls?" Henry looked at Lucy. "I think you know, don't you, Lucy?"

"You're the one who knows everything, it seems to me." Lucy looked at Henry as an aunt might look at a tiresome but adored nephew. "I told you in London that Eddie had never remarried, which was quite true. However, for many years he has found real companionship and"—she paused—"and solace with Melinda Murphy, who was his first-ever girlfriend. Ilicia is their daughter; she was born soon after Eddie went off to England and married Mavis." Lucy appealed to Henry. "You know that there's no stigma attached to such things in these parts. Anyhow, after Mavis died, Eddie went back to Melinda. She is a dear, charming, simple woman—but she would be appalled at the thought of taking on the job of Governor-General's wife, so they have never married. Everybody on Tampica knows about it, but we keep tactfully silent."

Smiling, Henry said, "That's what Chester Carruthers said."

"If she knew that Wright was DEA, why didn't she tell her father?" Emmy demanded.

"She must have been sworn to secrecy," Henry explained. "You see, Wright, in his capacity as a double-agent, was frightened of both of you, Lucy, and Sir Edward. He wanted all the information he could get about your goings-on, and he got it from Ilicia. He must have had his suspicions of me very early on—confirmed by Ilicia, owing to some incautious remark of Sir Edward's. It was certainly from her that he found out the code name by which I contacted Ironmonger at Melinda's Market. I imagine the fake message was actually phoned through by Porter."

"If Wright's original plan had succeeded," said Emmy, "it would have involved trapping Carruthers and Palmer and getting them sent to prison. Was Carmelita actually prepared to betray her own husband?"

"She hates him," said Lucy, simply. "She'll do anything for cocaine. Wright would have been a constant source of supply."

"When did Wright decide that Stevenson must be disposed of?" Lucy asked.

"Poor Stevenson was doomed from the start, I'm afraid," Henry told her. "Wright and Porter—who had nothing to do with the DEA, but was Wright's hireling—would have got rid of him somehow, but probably not until after the arrest of the two Tampicans. However, when he found out who I was, Wright decided to act at once."

"I don't see why." This from Emmy.

"Stevenson was no fool, and he was suspicious of me from the first. I'm sure now that he must have spotted us with Sir Edward on the beach that very first day—he was parasailing, you remember—and he undoubtedly heard from the terrace outside the dining room when Sir Edward appeared to recognize us for the first time. Also, he certainly saw us with Carruthers and Palmer at the Palmer house—again from his parasailing lookout. Now, Stevenson wasn't sure at that point whether or not Ironmonger was in cahoots with Carruthers and Palmer. Basically, he distrusted all the top men in the Tampican government. He must have thought that I was a genuine drug runner, who might ruin all his plans. Of course he confided his fears to his partner. That made it imperative for Wright to discover who I really was—and when he did, he realized that things were getting a little too hot. Stevenson had to be put out of action at once, and as for Emmy and myself—well, you know what he worked out for us." Henry turned to Pendleton. "I suppose he called on you when he came to the Seawards to bring Carmelita back from the clinic?"

"That's right. He turned up quite late in the evening, presented his credentials—which of course I checked with Washington—and told me that you were in Tampica and that it was important for the two of you to cooperate. I called London, who of course confirmed who you were. Wright might not have been one hundred percent certain of your identity up till then—but after that, there was no more doubt.

"Next day, after I'd heard about Stevenson's death, Wright radioed me—we listen out at Government House on the boating frequency—and told me in a roundabout way that he had to abort his mission and that you were taking over. It was very ingenious, and it might have worked."

"How did Carruthers find out that De Marco was really—?" Emmy began, and then answered her own question. "Of course. He told Carmelita to tell her husband, as if she'd just discovered it."

"Ironically," Henry said, "it was Wright himself who insisted I was too trusting when it came to other people. By the time I had worked out his connection with Carmelita and Ilicia, I was reasonably sure what he was up to—but it's no joking matter to accuse a fellow officer of treason. However, when I saw *Bellissima* back in the Seawards in time for my rendezvous with the Tampicans, I was convinced I was right. The only thing I could think of to do was to get in touch with Lucy."

"You might have warned me," put in Sir Alfred.

"Would you have believed me, sir?"

The Governor sighed. "I very much doubt it, Tibbett."

"Well, there you are."

"The thing that makes me mad," said Lucy, "is to think of Carruthers and Palmer going scot-free."

"I don't think they will," Henry said. "Wright is sure to

implicate them when he comes to trial—and think of the scandal that Carmelita's arrest will cause. At the very worst, those two will be finished in politics, and they'll be very lucky if they don't end up in jail."

"Leaving the field wide open for Commissioner Kelly?" asked Lucy acidly.

Surprisingly, Henry said, "I don't think Kelly is such a bad fellow. My guess is that once he knows he has nothing more to fear from Wright, he'll make a good Prime Minister. Eddie Ironmonger will keep a strict eye on him, and he's seen enough of the seamy side of the drug trade to put him off it for life, with any luck. His most difficult job will be to convince all the Tampicans who have been making a bit on the side that honest trading and bona fide tourism is the best way to make a living."

"Which reminds me," said Lucy. "I really must go and telephone the news to Eddie. You know, for a moment I almost suspected him of being mixed up in all this. Ignoble of me, but, as Henry says, in these situations one suspects even one's friends. That's the thing that makes it all so evil. Well, one of the things." She stood up. "Order my dinner for me, will you, Henry? Conch fritters and chocolate mousse. Shall I remember you to Eddie?"

"Please," said Henry. "And ask him to forgive me. I don't think I stand very high in his estimation at the moment."

"Don't worry," said Lucy. "You will."

EPILOGUE

It was a week later. The boring but majestic processes of the law were grinding on. The British Seaward Islands and the United States of America were wrangling amiably over which of them should have the pleasure of throwing the book at ex-Agent Wright. Randy Porter was being held on St. Mark's on charges of attempted murder and possession of an illegal firearm. There was no provable connection with drugs in his case. Carmelita Carruthers had been consigned by a merciful government to Dr. Duncan's clinic instead of to prison. Chester Carruthers had resigned as Prime Minister, and Joseph Palmer was on indefinite sick leave. Sir Edward Ironmonger had named a date for a general election. It was noticeable that quite a number of wealthy Tampicans had suddenly become fervent crusaders against drug abuse.

The Tibbetts had returned to Tampica and Pirate's Cave. It was likely that Emmy would have to come back to the Seawards to give evidence at Porter's trial, but meanwhile, there was no excuse to prolong their stay.

Dolphin, his self-confidence restored, was back at his old job at Pirate's Cave. The brilliant red, white, and blue of his parachute glided above the jewel-dark Caribbean as Henry and Emmy sat with Lucy on their balcony, having a farewell drink—the old lady having insisted on being driven over from Sugar Mill House to say good-bye.

Henry said, "Look here, Lucy. There's something worrying me. You told us in London that we'd get a special rate here at Pirate's Cave—but there's been no bill at all. Not for drinks or anything. It's ridiculous."

"I told you not to worry, you silly man. Everything is taken care of."

"If you mean that you are paying—"

"I'm paying nothing. Now, drink up, or you'll be late for your check-in time. Everything is so formal at the airport these days."

"And there's another thing," Henry persisted. "You told us that at one point you even suspected Eddie Ironmonger—and yet you never for a moment doubted that the manager here, Patrick Bishop, was absolutely honest and straight. And now there's no bill. Come on, Lucy. Explain."

For a moment, Lucy hesitated. Then, in her usual brisk voice, she said, "It's very simple, Henry. He is my son."

"Your—?" Emmy was speechless.

"Oh, it's a long time ago now. Dr. Duncan and I—well, you've often asked me why I never married. And of course he had his family—his Tampican wife and their children. I didn't feel I could call the boy Deacon, so we decided on Bishop. Quite a step up, ecclesiastically. So of course there's no bill. Now, come along. And don't ask so many questions."